The Mad Scientists' Club

by BERTRAND R. BRINLEY

Cover illustration by Leslie Morrill

SCHOLASTIC BOOK SERVICES
New York Toronto London Auckland Sydney Tokyo

*These stories are dedicated to all boys —
who like to dream about things they would
like to do — and to my agent, Carl Brandt,
without whose constant prodding I probably
never would have written them.*

The following three stories have appeared earlier in
Boys' Life: "The Unidentified Flying Man of Mam-
moth Falls," "The Strange Monster of Strawberry
Lake," and "Night Rescue."

ISBN: 0-590-32318-0

12 11 10 9 8 7 6 5 4 3 2 1   10   1 2 3 4 5 6/8

Printed in the U. S. A.   06

Contents

The Strange Sea Monster
of Strawberry Lake

Dinky Poore didn't really mean to start the story about the huge sea monster in Strawberry Lake. He was only telling a fib because he had to have an excuse for getting home late for supper. So he told his folks he'd been running around the lake trying to get a close look at a huge, snakelike thing he'd seen in the water, and the first thing he knew he was too far from home to get back in time.

His mother and father greeted this tale with some skepticism. But Dinky's two sisters were more impressionable, and that's how the story really got out. They kept pestering him for so many 'details about the monster that he had to invent a fantastic tale to satisfy them. That's one of the troubles with a lie. You've got to keep adding to it to make it believable to people.

It didn't take long for the story to get around town, and pretty soon Dinky Poore was a celebrity in Mammoth Falls. He even had his picture in the paper, together with an "artist's conception" of the thing he had seen. It was gruesome-looking — something like a dinosaur, but with a scaly, saw-toothed back like a dragon. Dinky was never short on imagination, and he was able to give the artist plenty of details.

It was the artist's sketch in the newspaper that got Henry Mulligan all excited. Henry is first vice-president and also chief of research for the Mad Scientists' Club and is noted for his brainstorms. Neither Henry nor anyone else in the club actually believed Dinky had seen a real monster, but we were all willing to play along with a gag — especially when Henry suggested that we could build a monster just like the one shown in the newspaper.

"Build a monster?" Freddy Muldoon's round face was all goggle-eyed. He liked the idea, but he just didn't know how Henry proposed going about it. He rubbed his button nose, which was

2

always itching, and asked, "You mean a real monster that can swim?"

"Don't be a dope," said Dinky.

"I'm not a dope. But who ever heard of a monster that can't swim?"

"The one we build will float," said Henry, rubbing his chin and looking up at the rafters of the club laboratory the way he always did when he was speculating on a new project. "All we need is some canvas and chicken wire, and Jeff Crocker's canoe."

Jeff Crocker is president of our club — mainly because his father owns the barn that we have our lab in, but also because he's just as smart as Henry and maybe a little more scientific. Henry dreams up most of the schemes that we get messed up in; but it is usually Jeff who figures out how to do everything, or how to get us out of what we got into.

Since Henry's plan to build a lake monster seemed like a good one, we held a formal meeting of the club that night to take a vote on it. Naturally, we all voted in favor of it, and three days later we had most of it finished. We built it on a small piece of dry land hidden 'way back in the swampy end of the lake. Henry and Jeff had designed a frame of light lumber and laths that

3

had the shape of a big land lizard, and we suspended this across the gunwales of the canoe. Then we hung chicken wire on the frame and stretched canvas over it. With a little paint and a few shiny tin can lids spotted here and there, we soon had a loathsome-looking creature guaranteed to scare the life out of anyone a hundred yards away from it.

Jeff had to keep putting the brakes on Henry's fancy ideas, but he did let him outfit the head with a pair of red eyes — which were just flashlights with red lenses stuck out through the canvas. Henry installed a switch and circuit breaker in the canoe, so that the "eyes" could be made to blink. After two days of practice back in the swamps we figured we could handle the beast well enough to make a test run out on the lake. The monster's profile stuck up about four feet out of the water, and it was a cinch for four of us to sit upright in the canoe to do the paddling and steering.

Meanwhile the town was still all excited about the possibility that there was a real, live sea monster in Strawberry Lake. A reporter from one of the big city papers had been in town to interview Dinky Poore, and when folks heard this, a lot of them began to recall seeing strange things on the water. Everybody wanted to get into the act, and pretty soon all sorts of people were volunteering information. Daphne Muldoon got her picture on the front page, not because she had seen the monster, but because she lived in Mammoth Falls and had a good-looking face and pretty legs. Daphne is one of Freddy Muldoon's cousins. Her younger brother, Harmon, used to be a member of our club. But he got kicked out for conduct unbecoming a scientist and for giving away secret information.

The first night we took the beast out was a Saturday, when the lake cabins and beachfront were crowded with weekend visitors. We figured it was best to wait until just before dark, then people couldn't see too well and there were fewer boats on the lake. There are plenty of small islands near the swampy end of Strawberry Lake, and this gave us a good chance to get the monster out into open water for a short run and then scoot it back into the cover of the swamp before anyone could discover where it had gone.

Homer Snodgrass, who is one of the brighter members of our club, had agreed to sit on the front porch of his folks' cabin so that we could get a firsthand report on what the monster looked like from the shore. Jeff and I were sitting in the middle of the canoe and doing the paddling. Mortimer Dalrymple, our electronics wizard, was steering; and Henry sat up in the prow, where he could look out through two peepholes.

"Are there many people on the beach?" Jeff asked.

"Scads of them," said Henry. "It's still light enough to see pretty well, but I don't think anybody has sighted us yet."

It was dark as black velvet inside the monster, though, and there was a damp, musty odor of canvas and paint. It was a little like being in the Tunnel of Love at an amusement park. I started to giggle, and Jeff told me to shut up or I might spoil everything. But I think he wanted to giggle too, and was afraid I might start him off.

"Don't get all shook up," came Mortimer's quiet voice from somewhere in the darkness back toward the monster's tail. Mortimer is always quiet like that. He never gets excited about anything. "It's half a mile over to the beach. They can't hear us unless we make a real big noise," he pointed out.

Suddenly Henry jumped violently, bumping his head on the framework of the beast's spine and rocking the canoe. "They've seen us," he cried. "They've seen us!"

6

"What? How do you know?" asked Jeff in a whisper.

"There's a whole bunch of them running out to the end of the boat dock. They're jumping up and down and pointing out here and waving and screaming."

Henry was right. We could hear some shouting now, and a few shrill screams of women.

"Let's rock the boat some!" Mortimer shouted from the back. "Give 'em a good show!" He was excited too, for once.

"I can't see anything now," Henry cried. "My glasses are all wet."

We could hear Henry moving around up front, as Mortimer started rocking the canoe from the rear and swishing the beast's huge tail back and forth through the water. Suddenly there was a splash and a gurgle, and my paddle hit something heavy and soft. Then there was a glurping noise, and something grabbed my paddle and tried to pull it out of my hands. There was a lot of thrashing going on, and I got scared and started hollering at Jeff to help me. The canoe and the whole framework of the monster were rocking violently.

"Maybe we've run into a real monster!" Mortimer snickered.

"Shut up and stop rocking," Jeff shouted. "Where's Henry?"

Just then Henry's head appeared right beside me, and one of his hands grasped the gunwale of the canoe. "Glurp," he said, "my glasses, I — lost 'em."

By this time Mortimer had stopped rocking and we managed to pull Henry back into the canoe.

"Get up front and see where we are," Jeff commanded, shoving me by the shoulder. "We've got to get this monster out of here before somebody starts chasing us in a motorboat. Henry, what were you doing in the water, anyway?"

Henry was choking on lake water, and didn't bother to answer.

When we got back into town that night we stopped in for a Coke and ice cream at Martin's Ice Cream Parlor, where Homer had agreed to meet us. The whole town was buzzing. Everybody in Martin's was talking about the sea monster, and about how Dinky Poore had been right, after all. We took a booth in a corner, where nobody could overhear us, and listened to Homer's report. There was no doubt the beast had been a sensational success. Homer said it had almost rolled over once and all the women on the beach had screamed. When Homer left the beach, state police cars had arrived and were sweeping the lake with their spotlights. But they didn't see anything, of course.

We took the monster out a couple more times that week, and got to be pretty expert at handling her. The town just about went wild. The newspaper offered a hundred dollars as a prize to anyone who could get a picture of the beast, and people started flocking into Mammoth Falls from all over the state, hoping to get a look at it. Lake cabins were renting for as high as two hundred dollars apiece, when they used to bring fifty a week; and a lot of local families just moved back into town and rented their cabins out to sightseers. All the concessions at the beach were doing a booming business, and the restaurants and the one hotel in town couldn't handle the crowds. Homer's father, who runs a hardware store, said he'd never seen such business.

Pretty soon we realized we had a tiger by the tail. Business was so good, and people in town were so happy, that we didn't dare stop taking the monster out, even though it was wearing us down.

We soon had something worse to worry about, however. Homer Snodgrass came running over to my house right after lunch one day, all breathless.

"Guess what?" said Homer.

"Guess what?" I asked.

"Give the club code word!" he said.

"Skinamaroo!" I said.

"The information you are about to receive is classified *confidential*," Homer panted. "You swear not to tell it to anyone not a member of the Mad Scientists' Club?"

"I swear!"

Then Homer told me that Harmon Muldoon had been in his father's store with two men. They wanted ammunition for an elephant gun. Mr. Snodgrass doesn't carry that kind of ammunition, of course, but he did tell them where they could order it in Chicago. The two men were from out of town, and they said Harmon had promised to show them an island in the lake where they could set up a campsite and try to get a good shot at the monster when it came out in the evening. They decided to drive to Chicago to pick up the ammunition.

This news called for an emergency meeting of the club in executive session, and we held it that night in Jeff's barn. Everyone agreed that we couldn't take the beast out again and risk being shot through the head with an elephant gun. But Homer argued that we couldn't disappoint all the merchants and other people in town who were making money on the tourists. Dinky Poore, as usual, was in favor of writing a letter to the President and asking for his help.

While we were arguing, Henry Mulligan suddenly turned his eyes up toward the rafters and started stroking his chin. Whenever this happens, everybody stops talking and waits for Henry to speak. After a decent interval of respectful silence, Henry brought his eyes down and fixed them on Jeff.

"Your father has a small outboard motor that can be mounted on the canoe, hasn't he?"

"Sure," said Jeff. "We use it for fishing at the shallow end of the lake."

"And it's a pretty quiet one, as I remember?"

"It doesn't even scare the fish."

"O.K.," said Henry. "Now, if Homer can bamboozle his father out of a few essential pieces of hardware, I think we have enough equipment here in the lab to rig that motor up so that it can be controlled by radio. Then all we have to do is pick a good spot on the shore for our transmitters — on one of those steep hills on the north side — and we can make the beast do anything we want it to."

"And those hunters can shoot at it all they want, and they won't do anything more than put a few holes in the canvas," observed Mortimer.

"Jeepers," said Dinky, "I bet that'll make Harmon mad!"

In about a week we had most of the club's radio gear rigged up in the canoe so that we could make Jeff's outboard motor speed up, slow down, idle, turn right or left, and reverse itself. We made a few short test runs with it 'way back in the swamp end of the lake, and everything worked fine. This time Jeff agreed to letting Henry add a pump that would squirt water out of the beast's nostrils. And he even gave in to another of Henry's brainstorms. Freddy could make a bellow that sounded like a bull moose on a rampage, because his voice was beginning to change. So Henry figured it would be a good idea to install a loudspeaker in the belly of the monster and let Freddy bellow into a microphone once in a while from the place where we hid the transmitting equipment.

The first trip of the motorized monster was a sensation. Homer and Dinky and I couldn't see much of it, because it was our job to go back in the swamp, get the beast from its hiding place, and start the motor. Then we called Jeff on our walkie-talkie and he directed the operation from the wooded hill where we had our transmitting apparatus. Henry and Mortimer operated the radio controls to steer the beast and make the eyes blink and the nostrils spout water. Freddy stood by to bellow whenever Jeff tapped him on the shoulder. Jeff watched the monster all the time through binoculars.

She moved through the water much faster now, and every time Freddy let out with the bull-moose call it echoed back and forth among the hills and caused a regular panic on the beach. We got her back into the protection of the swamp just before dark, all right; but we had some anxious moments when she passed the last island out in open water. Four or five shots were fired at her, and Jeff said he could see the bullets splashing in the water. But the beast kept on going as though nothing had happened, and this must have caused Harmon's hunter friends some consternation.

The next day every newspaper in the country must have carried the story. They quoted eyewitnesses who swore that the monster was mad about something, because it was swimming a lot faster and making a frightening noise. A scientist in New York speculated that it might be the mating season for the beast, and suggested the possibility that there might actually be two of them. Within three days there must have been a hundred and fifty reporters in Mammoth Falls from newspapers, magazines, and radio and television stations. Newsreel camera crews were lined up along the beach, and several of them had large searchlights ready to sweep across the surface of the lake at dusk, when the monster usually appeared.

We kept the beast under wraps for a few days, and spent the time visiting with the camera crews and reporters. Most of them were camped on the beach, sleeping in cars and station wagons, because there weren't any rooms available in town. Besides getting a good line on what the reporters were planning to do, we were able to make a little money for the club treasury by running errands for them and operating a lemonade stand. Hot dogs were selling for thirty cents apiece at the beach, and for fifteen cents in town. We did a pretty good business buying them at Martin's Ice Cream Parlor and running them out to the beach in thermos jugs on our bicycles. Freddy Muldoon was able to get five dollars for an old telescope he bought for a dollar ninety-five through a magazine ad, and Henry traded some of his father's shaving cream for flash bulbs and camera film. We kept Dinky Poore's mother pretty busy making cakes and pies; but we didn't make much money on this venture, because Dinky and Freddy would eat up most of the profit. They also drank too much lemonade, and after the first day Jeff wouldn't let them run the stand any more.

By this time several of the reporters had made camp on the same island the hunters had been on, and rented some high-powered motorboats. They were determined to get close enough to the monster to get some good pictures. There were also a lot of people tramping around the shore every day, trying to get back into the swampy end of the lake. So we decided to move the beast to a new hiding place.

We picked out a deep cove studded with rocks and small islands, about two miles east of the swamp. Late at night, long after the searchlights had been turned off and people had gone to sleep, we towed the monster over there with a rowboat. Early the next morning, before the sun had come up, we took her out for a brief appearance on the lake and caught everybody by surprise. Some early-morning watchers on the beach started shouting, and this woke up a few of the reporters on the island. But the monster was not where they expected her to be, and by the time some of them had scrambled into their boats we had her back into the cove and covered up among a jumble of rocks.

This created quite a lot of confusion, and people began to believe the professor who had claimed there might be two monsters. But we could see that the string was running out for us. There were so many people exploring the lake now, and so many "scientific expeditions" on their way to investigate the "phenomenon," as they called it, that we were pretty sure somebody would discover our hiding place sooner or later. Even though most people were too scared to take boats out any more, there were several boats making regular patrols of the lake, and every once in a while a helicopter would fly over it.

We held a meeting to discuss the situation. Dinky Poore argued that Abraham Lincoln said you couldn't fool all of the people all of the time, and we might as well quit while we were ahead and claim the hundred-dollar reward the newspaper was offering. But Henry claimed that P. T. Barnum had proved Lincoln was wrong, and so had a lot of politicians. Homer Snodgrass was in favor of continuing as long as we could, because all the extra tourist business was good for the town, and Mammoth Falls had always been a pretty poor place. But Mortimer and Jeff and I were beginning to feel that we should confess the whole business to Mayor Scragg, because he was getting worried about the monster making the lake unsafe for boating and swimming. We also felt that Harmon Muldoon would get wise to us pretty soon and spill the beans. We had seen him sneaking around the lab a lot lately, and trying to follow us sometimes. We knew Harmon was a pretty bright boy. He had been our radio expert when he was in the club, and he had enough brains to figure out the whole deal eventually.

Freddy wasn't around when the meeting started, but he came busting in now, all out of breath after running all the way from his house. "The jig is up, fellas," he announced. "I think Harmon has snitched on us!"

We all started questioning Freddy at once, of course, and Jeff had to rap for order so that we could get the story straight. It seems that Harmon had been up early in the morning, fiddling with his ham radio outfit, and had picked up Freddy's bellow coming over the air. He recognized it as the sound the monster made, and he knew that it couldn't get on the air unless the monster was sitting next to a microphone.

"Holy smoke!" said Mortimer, slapping himself on the forehead. "We should have had brains enough to change all our frequencies after Harmon left the club. He knows which ones we use."

Freddy explained that Harmon had then gone to the local newspaper and told a reporter what he suspected, in the hopes of claiming the reward. The editors didn't intend to print his story until they had more proof, but they were certainly going to investigate his theory. Freddy got all this information from his father, who works in the composing room.

It didn't take us long to make a decision after getting this news. Mortimer had made good friends with one of the out-of-town reporters on the beach. His name was Bud Stewart and he wrote for the *Cleveland Plain Dealer*, which we knew was a big newspaper. So Jeff and Mortimer went to see him, and told him the story after he had agreed to a proposition. He got his home office to agree to buy the club an oscilloscope and a ten-channel transmitter for our lab, in return for exclusive pictures of the monster. Then we all sat down with Mr. Stewart and mapped out a plan of action.

Early the next morning we took him to our hiding place and uncovered the monster for him so he could take pictures of it. He also wanted to get some pictures of the beast in action, of course, so we planned to take it out for an excursion that very night. We figured that if we waited any longer Harmon Muldoon would have time to show the local newspaper people how to get a fix on the location of our transmitters by tuning in our frequency from two or three different places. Mr. Stewart went out to the airport to hire a helicopter. He planned to fly over the lake just before dusk, and when we saw him we were to unleash the monster.

That night we were all in our positions early, just in case Mr. Stewart misjudged the time. It seemed like a long wait, but he finally appeared and waved to us from the helicopter. We had the beast all ready and started her out to the open water. Those of us who had to stay back in the cove couldn't see what happened next, but we could tell, from all the shouts and the way the helicopter was flying, that this was the monster's most triumphant appearance. We got all the details later, including a look at Mr. Stewart's pictures.

The reporters who were camped on the island

were ready for us this time, and three boatloads of them appeared as soon as the monster got out there. They had newsreel cameras mounted in the boats, and they were only about half a mile from the beast when Jeff gave the order to head her back to the cove. But Henry couldn't make her do a tight enough turn, and she started back on the far side of a large island that lay across the mouth of the cove. This island is a huge granite mountaintop that rises up out of the water as high as a hundred feet in some places. Once the beast got behind this mass, Henry lost contact with her, and for a few moments she was running free. For some reason the monster doubled back on its tracks, and to everyone's amazement shot out from behind the island again, heading straight for the boats of the pursuing cameramen. Incredibly, the beast suddenly gained speed and went roaring full throttle at the tiny boats — now less than a quarter of a mile away.

The newspaper men in the boats had been busy signaling their crewmen on the shore to turn on the big searchlights, and they didn't notice that the monster had reversed its course until it had closed almost half the gap between them. When they did turn to see it bearing down on them, with nostrils spouting spray and the red eyes blinking, panic broke loose among them. All three boats suddenly turned to head back for the safety of the beach. One of them nearly collided with another and had to turn so sharply that it capsized, spilling its occupants and its gear into the lake. There had been five men in the boat, and when they rose to the surface they swam frantically for the nearest island.

Henry and Mortimer, meanwhile, were pushing buttons and flipping switches so fast that the two of them looked like a centipede with a case of poison ivy. But no matter what they did they couldn't regain control of the beast. Suddenly Mortimer shouted, "Harmon Muldoon must be transmitting on our frequency, and he's got a stronger signal than we have! He's got the thing jammed at full throttle. Cut the receiver, Henry!"

Henry threw the emergency switch that cut off the power supply to the main receiver inside the beast. She slowed down so suddenly that the head almost went under water. Freddy was so excited that he gave out with a big "Hooray!" that sounded like the battle cry of a raging bull elephant. You could hear the screams of the people on the beach, as they heard it come out of the loudspeaker.

"Switch to the alternate receiver now!" cried

Mortimer, and Henry did so. This one operated on a different frequency, and Mortimer had insisted on installing it in case something went wrong with the main one. Since Harmon Muldoon couldn't know we were changing frequencies, it was not very likely he could jam this one too.

The beast started back toward the cove like a docile cow coming home for supper, and the searchlights on the beach came on, finally. But all that the watchers on the shore could see was the tail of the beast disappearing in the darkness.

It was about two hours later that we met Mr. Stewart at Martin's Ice Cream Parlor to discuss what we should do next. The local radio station had just announced that Mayor Scragg had asked the Governor to get the Navy to fire depth charges in the lake in the hope of killing the monster. The reporters and cameramen stranded on the little island had been rescued by a police launch, but they were mad as wet hens and had apparently convinced the Mayor that the beast was a menace to the public health and safety.

We went back out to the lake that night and stripped all our equipment out of the beast, including Jeff Crocker's canoe. We mounted her frame on an old raft that someone had abandoned on the shore. Then we towed her far enough out in the lake so that she would be visible from the shore in the morning, and anchored her there. We hung a wreath of pine cones on her neck, and Henry and Mortimer rigged up some kind of a diabolical device inside her.

As soon as it was light in the morning we all climbed up to the place on the hillside where our transmitters were located. We could see a few people on the beach looking at the beast through binoculars, but nobody was taking any boats out. When the sun started to peep over the ridge at the east end of the lake, Henry pushed a button and a lot of smoke came billowing out of the monster. All of a sudden she burst into flames that climbed about thirty feet high, and a big column of black smoke went up into the sky. When the smoke had cleared away there was nothing left on the lake but a dirty smear of oil and a few pieces of black debris — and that was the last that anyone ever saw of the strange sea monster of Strawberry Lake.

We packed up our gear and started for home; and Dinky Poore, who is the youngest member of the Mad Scientists' Club, started to cry a little bit as we were trudging through the woods. Since the monster had really been his idea in the beginning, I guess he felt as though he had lost a close relative. But Jeff told him he could have two votes the next time the club had a meeting, and he had stopped blubbering by the time we got home.

The Big Egg

If Harmon Muldoon had been sneaking around the Mad Scientists' clubhouse one night last August, he would have seen the whole bunch of us sitting around the table staring at a grisly-looking object about the size of a football. As events turned out, he probably was, because we aren't sure to this day whether there isn't a prehistoric creature roaming around the swamps north of Strawberry Lake.

"How old did you say that thing was, Henry?" asked Freddy Muldoon. Freddy was staring bug-eyed at the thing, with his elbows on the table and his fingers pushing his fat cheeks up around his eyeballs.

"It's probably about a hundred and fifty mil-

25

lion years old, give or take a few million years," said Henry Mulligan.

Freddy's eyes bulged larger. "There isn't anything that old," he said. "That's older'n Methuselah!"

"That's right!" said Henry, matter-of-factly.

"What on earth are we going to do with it?" mused Dinky Poore, blinking his eyes and yawning.

"I don't know yet," said Henry, as he wiped his glasses. "I've got an idea, but I want to do a lot more research first."

"In that case, I think I'll go home to bed," said Dinky, slipping off his stool.

"Me too!" said Freddy Muldoon.

Whenever Henry says he has an idea, we know it's time to start catching up on sleep. He'd had us out all day digging for fossils in the old quarry back in the high hills west of the lake, and we were all dog-tired. We picked up the greenish-gray object that was sitting on the table and packed it carefully in a box of sawdust. Henry ran his hand slowly over its crusty surface before we put the lid on.

"Better lock it in the safe," he said.

Then we all went home to ponder over the thing that Henry said was a dinosaur egg. Dinky

Poore had a good point. After all, what do you do with a dinosaur egg besides look at it?

But while the rest of us slept that hot August night, Henry Mulligan was very busy. What he was up to, none of us would have imagined in our wildest dreams. And it set in motion a chain of events that still has everyone in town confused.

"Hey, gang, I've got a great idea!" cried Dinky Poore, as he burst into the clubhouse the next day. "Why don't we set up a tent in Homer's front yard and charge ten cents a peek to look at the egg?"

"Crazy!" said Freddy Muldoon, who was munching sunflower seeds in the corner. "I'll bet we could almost make a million. Everybody in town would want to see it."

But Homer Snodgrass shook his head. "I've got a better idea," he said to Dinky. "Why don't we put the tent in *your* front yard and charge two bits?"

"My old man wouldn't like it. That's why!"

"That's parents for you," said Freddy, with his chin in his hand. "Always standing in the way of progress."

"You've got the wrong idea," said Henry, quietly. "This is a scientific curiosity. It may be an important discovery. You don't make money from a thing like that. Everybody's got a right to see it, and it's our duty to let the scientific world know about it."

"I guess that's why there are no rich scientists," said Freddy Muldoon.

Henry unlocked the safe and brought out the egg. It looked strangely different in the daylight, somehow. Not half so grisly.

"It seems a lot lighter than it did last night," said Dinky Poore, as he took it out of the box and laid it on the table.

"That's because you were tired," said Henry, "and we had to carry it a long way. You're stronger this morning."

"I guess so," said Dinky, feeling both his muscles. Dinky is always feeling his muscles, because he has the smallest ones in the club. Come to think of it, I guess that's why Freddy is always rubbing his belly. He has the biggest stomach in the club. Dinky's always wishing his muscles would get bigger, and Freddy's always wishing his waistline would shrink.

We helped Henry develop the pictures we had taken of the egg the night before, and we put them in a package with the loose shell fragments we had found near it. Mortimer Dalrymple, who is the only member of our club who can make the typewriter work, typed out all the dimensions and the weight of the egg, and Henry ran off to the post office to mail the whole works to some museum in New York City that he said knew all about dinosaurs. When he got back he told us what he thought we should do with the egg.

"I guess we'll have to give it to some museum," he said, "because it might turn out to be an important discovery, but I'd like to conduct a little experiment first."

"What's that?" asked Mortimer.

"I think we ought to try and hatch it!" said Henry.

Jeff Crocker dropped his gavel on the floor and strode over to open the door and let a little air into the clubhouse.

"Henry, as president of this club, I want to know if you've gone off your rocker?" he said.

"You mean hatch a real dinosaur?" asked Dinky Poore.

"What else would come out of a dinosaur egg?" Henry observed.

"That egg doesn't look very fresh to me," said Homer, looking at it critically.

Jeff Crocker mopped his brow and sat down again. "Henry, I thought you said this thing was over a hundred and fifty million years old?"

"It probably is. But the sand around the Salton Sea is full of shrimp eggs that are over two thousand years old. You can buy them in hobby shops and in chemistry sets. All you do is put them in water and they'll hatch in twenty-four hours. If an egg doesn't die in two thousand years, when does it die?"

"When it stinks!" said Homer Snodgrass.

Dinky bent over and sniffed the big egg. "It does smell kind of funny," he said.

"What on earth do you feed a real dinosaur?" asked Freddy Muldoon.

About an hour later we were trudging through the low swamps that wind among the hills north of Strawberry Lake. This was where we had hidden the lake monster when we were building it. Almost nobody ever goes there except berry pickers, and there are a lot of places that nobody has ever explored. I guess we know the swamps as well as anybody, and even we don't ever venture into the more remote areas.

We were picking our way carefully along a tangled path that wound around the bottom of a hill, when all of a sudden some rocks came tumbling down the slope and we heard something scurrying off through the bushes. Jeff crept up through the undergrowth and took a look around, but said he couldn't see anything.

"Must have been a fox," he speculated.

"Maybe it was a member of the IES spying on us," said Mortimer Dalrymple.

"What's the IES?" asked Freddy, his eyes bulging.

"That's the International Egg Syndicate," said Mortimer in a low voice. "They're a dangerous band of criminals that specialize in stealing dinosaur eggs from museums and selling them to private collectors all over the world."

"Oh, knock it off, Mortimer!" Jeff muttered. "You read too many kooky books and watch all the wrong TV shows."

"Well, you can't be too careful these days," said Mortimer. "There're all kinds of international agents running around in the bushes."

Henry led us to a boggy area deep in the recesses of the swamp where a spit of pure white sand jutted out from the tail end of a small hill. It was mostly covered with blueberry bushes, but Henry picked out a sandy clearing near the bog and we buried the big egg there near the water, about a foot deep in the sand. We drew some lines in the sand to the edge of the clearing and placed stone markers there so we could locate the exact spot again.

"How long does it take a big egg like that to hatch?" asked Dinky.

"Nobody knows," said Henry. "That's one of the things we aim to find out. It would be an important contribution to paleontology."

"Watch your language!" said Freddy Muldoon. "I heard that."

"Would it take a year?" asked Dinky.

"Nobody knows," said Henry.

Dinky and Freddy weren't about to wait a year, however. They were back out in the swamp the next day to check on the egg, and when they got back into town they ran all over looking for the rest of us. They found Jeff and me at Henry's house, helping him wash the family car.

"The egg's gone!" Freddy cried, as soon as he spied us.

"It 'steriously disappeared!" chimed in Dinky.

"Is that so?" Henry said, cool as a cucumber.

"How do you know?" Jeff asked them.

"We dug it up, and it's not there."

"How could you dig it up, if it isn't there?" Henry asked, still scrubbing a tire.

"Aw, c'mon, Henry. You know what I mean," said Freddy, kicking the tire and getting his dirty fingers all over the trunk of the car.

"I'll bet Harmon Muldoon stole it," said Dinky, jumping up and down. "I'll bet it was him out there in the bushes that kicked those rocks down."

32

"Maybe we'd better go out there," said Jeff, looking at Henry.

"I suppose so," Henry answered. "Hand me that other brush."

"Well, let's get going," said Dinky, impatiently. "This old car can wait."

"Tomorrow morning'll be time enough," said Henry, as he hosed down the front of the car. "If the egg's already gone, nobody can steal it."

"Tomorrow morning?" Freddy exclaimed. "Aw, nuts! You gonna fiddle while Rome burns, I suppose!"

"Who's burning, besides you?" said Henry, spraying him with the hose.

"O.K., you old fiddler crab!" said Freddy.

The next morning we did make our way out to the sandpit again, but everything seemed to be normal. The markers we had left were still in place and the ground looked undisturbed.

"Somebody's been out here again!" said Dinky. "Freddy and I dug a big hole right there, looking for the egg, and somebody has filled it in."

"Well, let's just see if the egg is here now," said Jeff.

We drew lines out from the markers and started digging at the point where they intersected. The egg was there, all right, just as we'd left it, though it didn't look as though it had made much progress toward hatching. Everyone turned and looked at Dinky and Freddy.

"What's the idea, bringing us 'way out here on a wild-goose chase?" Mortimer snorted at them. "We've got more important things to do."

"If this is your idea of a joke, you two'll never make a living as comedians," said Jeff. "We oughta toss you in the swamp."

Little Dinky started to blubber. "Honest Injun, Jeff. Somebody has been out here. There wasn't any egg there when Freddy and I were here yesterday."

"Scout's honor!" said Freddy, giving the sign.

"Maybe you dug in the wrong place. You guys don't dig things too well, you know," said Mortimer sarcastically.

"Maybe we did. But who filled our hole up?" said Dinky, kicking sand at him. His voice was all choked up, and there was a big tear running down the left side of his face.

"How do I know? Maybe the whole thing was in your head," Mortimer jibed at him.

While they were arguing, I noticed that Henry had lifted the big egg out of the hole and was examining it closely with his pocket magnifying

34

glass. There was a mysterious smile on his face as he placed it back in the sand.

"What's so funny, Henry? Can you see the dinosaur in there already?" I asked him.

Henry started, as though he hadn't realized anyone was looking at him. "Everything's fine, Charlie. Just fine," he said, and covered the egg up with sand.

But everything wasn't "just fine" as far as Dinky and Freddy were concerned. Dinky moped all the way home; and later he and Freddy told me they were certain the egg had been missing when they had tried to dig it up the day before.

"We think my cousin Harmon has been up to something, and we aim to find out what he's doing," Freddy explained.

"We've got to prove to the other guys that we're not nuts," Dinky added.

I felt sorry for both of them, and I agreed to help out in setting a watch on Harmon's clubhouse. This wasn't difficult, because Harmon's gang always meets on the second story of an old garage in back of Stony Martin's house. It faces Egan's Alley, and across the alley and just a little way down is the old Blaisdell barn. The Blaisdells are an old couple that can't run very fast, and they long ago got tired of trying to chase us out of their loft. Old man Blaisdell just decided to buy more insurance and relax, and we've had the run of the place ever since.

It's a neat place to spy from. There's windows at both ends of the loft, and there's a cupola on top that you can climb up into and look out through the ventilation slits. From it we could keep a good watch on Stony Martin's garage.

That night we saw Stony come out and dump a bucketful of stuff into a trash can in the alley. It sounded like rocks. Then he chipped away at the inside of the bucket with a screwdriver and washed it out with a hose. After he went back inside the garage, Dinky couldn't contain his curiosity any longer. He sneaked across the alley and shinnied up a telephone pole so he could peek inside the lighted window on the second floor. We held our breath, hoping nobody would come out and see him there. Suddenly we saw him swing over onto the sloping roof of the garage and lie flat against it. Harmon came to the lighted window and raised the sash so he could look out into the alley. He took a good look around, then pulled his head in and closed the window again. We breathed easier, but Dinky lay motionless on the roof, pressing himself against the shingles. Pretty soon the light went out, and we could hear them clumping down the stairs inside. Harmon and Stony came out the back door, locked it behind them, and disappeared down the alley.

As soon as they were out of sight, Dinky scrambled down the pole and came running pell-mell toward Blaisdell's barn. We met him halfway down the ladder from the loft.

"They've got our egg!" he said in a breathless whisper. "I saw it sitting on a table up there."

We dashed across the alley and Dinky shinnied up the pole again. He jumped onto the roof of the garage and let himself down over the eaves onto the windowsill. The window was unlocked, and it took him only a second to scramble inside. Then he groped his way down the stairs in the dark and unlatched the alley door. I slipped inside with him while Freddy kept watch behind one of the trash cans in the alley.

Dinky's flashlight picked out the table against the wall, and sure enough, there was the big egg sitting unprotected in the middle of it. We looked around for something to wrap it in and found a pile of burlap bags in one corner. I pulled a couple of them off the top of the pile and felt something hard under the next bag. Pulling it aside, I shined my flashlight onto what looked like a couple of small wash basins. Dinky stood beside me, breathing hard.

"What are those, Charlie? They look like big hunks of plaster."

"I think I know," I said. "And I think they can tell us a lot about what's been going on."

We got the big egg off the table and fitted it into the depression in one of the chunks of plaster. It fitted perfectly.

"These are plaster molds," I whispered. "Are you thinking what I'm thinking?"

"Yeah! That's what Stony was throwing away in the ash can. Old chunks of plaster of Paris."

"Yes! But don't you see? These are two halves of a plaster mold made from our dinosaur egg. What would they make a mold for?"

"To make another egg," said Dinky.

"Exactly! And that's what's out in the swamp right now — a fake egg made out of plaster of Paris and painted up."

"I wonder why they'd do that?" Dinkey hissed.

"So they could claim they found the egg, instead of us, and get all the credit. That Harmon would do anything; but this time he's gonna get fooled."

"Whatcha gonna do?"

38

"We're going to beat them at their own game," I said. "We're gonna switch eggs on them, and they'll never know the difference."

We wrapped the egg in a couple of burlap bags and beat it out of there, being careful to leave the door unlocked. It took us about two hours to get out to the right place in the swamps, find the fake egg in the darkness, and put the real egg back in its place. Then it took us another two hours to get back to Egan's Alley. Our hearts were thumping pretty loudly when we tiptoed up the creaky stairs of Stony's garage again; but it was well after midnight, and we figured we were pretty safe as long as we didn't make any noise. Since we found the door still unlocked, we were pretty sure nobody had discovered the egg was missing.

When we got to the top of the stairs, we groped our way carefully to the table. I reached out for the edge of it and almost screamed out loud when my hand came down on what felt like another human hand.

"It's about time you got back," said a voice. "What took you so long?"

Dinky jumped back clear to the top of the stairs and snapped his flashlight on. My heart had stopped, but it started beating again when I saw that the figure sitting at the end of the table was Henry Mulligan.

For a minute I had all sorts of wild thoughts. What was Henry doing here in Harmon Muldoon's clubhouse? Was he in cahoots with Harmon for some reason? How did he know what we were up to?

"Jeepers, Henry, you scared the daylights out of us," said Dinky.

"What on earth are you doing here?" I asked, when I could find my voice.

"Never mind," said Henry. "Put the egg back, and let's get out of here!"

"This isn't the real egg," said Dinky. "We found the real one here and took it back out to the swamp."

"I know all about where you've been," Henry said quietly. "You just had to prove you were right, didn't you? Now put the egg down and let's scram."

I propped the egg up on the table, just where we'd found the other one, and we cleared out of there. At least Dinky and Freddy had vindicated themselves. And even though we didn't know exactly what Harmon was up to, we figured we were a step ahead of him. The big question, though, was Henry Mulligan's strange behavior.

And it became even stranger during the next several days.

He seemed to spend hours and hours in the clubhouse, fiddling around with our ham radio set, and he wouldn't even talk about dinosaurs or let anyone go out to check on the egg. "The egg is all right," he would say. "Don't worry about it." Finally, one day, we talked him into going fishing, and we all got on our bicycles and rode 'way up into the hills to a favorite stream of ours. Henry didn't catch any fish, though. He almost never does. Somehow or other it seems that really smart people just don't attract fish. I think they just get bored with it all and aren't patient enough.

By early afternoon, Henry had talked us all into going back to town. When we got back to his house there was a man sitting on the porch waiting to see him. He introduced himself as a science reporter for one of the big city newspapers.

"I'm Mr. Bowden from the *Globe-Democrat*," he said. "I'd like to ask you a few questions about this big egg you found."

"What big egg?" asked Freddy Muldoon.

"The big egg that's supposed to be a dinosaur egg," said Mr. Bowden.

"Oh, that egg!" said Freddy. "You'll have to

talk to Henry Mulligan about that. He's our chief scientist."

"Thank you," Mr. Bowden said politely. "He's the one I came to talk to."

By this time Jeff had gotten hold of one of Freddy's ears and pulled him off to the side. Mr. Bowden explained that the American Museum of Natural History in New York had made fluorine tests on the shell fragments we sent them and were of the opinion that they were from the Jurassic period of the Mesozoic era. They thought the egg was probably that of a large sauropod dinosaur — possibly a brontosaurus, or maybe even a brachiosaurus. They were quite excited about it and had asked an expert from the state university to come down to Mammoth Falls to examine the egg. That was why Mr. Bowden was here. There would probably be reporters from other papers coming down with the expert.

"Who is he?" Henry asked.

"He's Professor Mudgeon, a very well-known paleontologist," said Mr. Bowden. "He'll be here tomorrow."

"What's all this stuff about the jackass period and all that?" asked Dinky Poore.

"That's *Jurassic*," said Henry. "All it means is that the egg is probably a hundred and fifty million years old, like I said."

The next day we all went over to the town hall to meet Professor Mudgeon, who had agreed to hold a press conference there. Mayor Scragg was there, of course. Whenever there's anything going on in Mammoth Falls that might get into the newspapers, you'll always find him in the middle of it. Today he was in great form, beaming and smiling, and patting Henry on the head as he introduced him to Professor Mudgeon. Henry kept ducking, trying to keep from getting his hair mussed, because he always figures a scientist should look as dignified as possible. Professor Mudgeon didn't look too dignified, though. His suit was a little rumpled, and his shirt collar was a little dirty, and he had bright, shining eyes that twinkled behind his thick-lensed glasses. And he had enough hair to make up for all that Mayor Scragg was lacking, and then some.

"We're very proud of these young men," said Mayor Scragg, mussing Henry's hair again.

"Well, I'm sure you should be," said Professor Mudgeon. "They may have made an important discovery." He had a habit of sucking air in through his teeth with a slurping sound after every statement, and then laughing with his teeth still closed.

After everybody had sat down, the professor gave a brief explanation of why he was there, and

43

told the reporters something about dinosaur fossils. In answer to a reporter's question, he explained the various methods scientists use to determine the age of fossils or bones. When he got to the uranium method, of course, the reporter from the Mammoth Falls *Gazette* had to get up and ask him if this egg was radioactive, and if there would be any danger to the community.

"No! I hardly think so," said the professor, laughing through his teeth again.

"What a dope that reporter is," said Henry, under his breath.

"When do we get to see the egg?" another reporter asked.

"Well, that's up to these young men here," said the professor, looking toward Henry. "I haven't seen it, myself, yet. As a matter of fact, I don't even know where it is."

"We buried it," said Henry, nonchalantly.

"Buried it? What for?"

"To see if it would hatch."

This brought the house down. Even the professor was laughing — with his mouth open this time. Then a second laugh broke out when the *Gazette* reporter asked if there was any remote possibility that the egg *might* hatch, and a live dinosaur be born.

"No, of course not!" said the professor, laughing openly again. Then suddenly his face clouded and the scientist in him reasserted itself. "On the other hand, I don't really know," he said seriously. "Things like that are decided by an authority greater than I."

Mayor Scragg was in such an expansive mood that he volunteered the services of both the town police department and the fire department to transport everybody out to a point where we could walk into the swamps. He even lent the professor a pair of leather puttees that he had left over from World War I. All the way out there he kept telling the professor what an important place Mammoth Falls was for geological exploration, and the professor kept saying, "Very interesting. Very interesting indeed!"

A lot of other people who hadn't been invited came trailing along after us, and we noticed Harmon and some of the members of his gang among them. Dinky Poore, of course, had to run out ahead of everybody so he could be the one to show the professor where the egg was; and when the rest of us rounded the end of the little hill where the sandpit jutted into the swamp, he came dashing back through the bushes shouting, "The egg has hatched! The dinosaur has gone!"

Sure enough, when the rest of us got to the little clearing, all we saw were broken fragments of what once had been the big egg, lying in a shallow pit in the sand. Professor Mudgeon stopped at the edge of the clearing and asked everyone to stand back. He looked at the ground very carefully, and then he tiptoed over to the edge of the bog where a series of tiny depressions were visible in the wet sand. He straightened up and drew a large magnifying glass from his coat pocket. Then he bent down and studied the depressions very closely.

They certainly looked like the footprints of some unknown kind of animal. They were shaped a little bit like an acorn with three sharp little points at the top — or maybe more like the profile of a slightly deformed tulip, just opening up. There were smaller prints interspersed among them that looked like an empty acorn shell upside down. They proceeded in a wavering line along the short stretch of shore, and then disappeared in the bushes, where the sand was drier.

After studying them for a while, and shaking his head from side to side, the professor moved over to where the big chunks of broken eggshell lay in the pit and picked up one or two of them. Finally he snorted and rose to his feet.

"Very clever! Very clever!" he said. "But a complete fake!"

Mayor Scragg harrumphed loudly, and a babble of noise and excited questions broke loose from the reporters. Over it all I was sure I could hear the sound of Harmon Muldoon's laughter. To back up his statement, the professor picked up one of the egg fragments, crumbled it to a white powder between his fingers, and tasted it.

"Pure plaster of Paris!" he snorted, spitting it out.

Mayor Scragg had turned purple and his cheeks were bellowing in and out. He glared at Henry Mulligan and the rest of us. Then he looked back at the professor and harrumphed again. Professor Mudgeon had moved over to look again at the footprints in the sand.

"Somebody has done a very clever job of duplicating the footprints of an infant brontosaurus," he said, "but he forgot one thing. The brontosaurus had a long, heavy tail that he could barely lift off the ground, and there is no trace of a tail being dragged along the ground here." Then he turned toward Mayor Scragg. "I'm very sorry, Mr. Mayor. But I must also say that I'm a little disappointed at coming all the way down here to be victimized by a fraud and a hoax!"

"You don't know the half of it!" spouted the Mayor, turning all purple again. "I'm very sorry too, Professor Mudhen, but if you had to live in a town full of teenage Machiavellis you might be able to appreciate what I'm up against."

"Mudgeon!" said the professor.

"What's that?"

"Mudgeon!" he repeated. "My name is Mudgeon!"

"Oh yes! Of course! *Very* sorry!" said Mayor Scragg.

"That's quite all right. I'm used to it," said the professor.

Several of the reporters were now taking photographs of the footprints and the egg fragments. A couple of others were trying to get information out of Henry, but he wasn't talking. "I'm not ready to make any statements," he told them, and walked over to where we were standing.

"What's going on?" Jeff asked him. "Is that our egg, or isn't it?" But Henry just shrugged his shoulders and moved away from us.

"It looks like you guys goofed," said Jeff, turning to glare at Dinky and Freddy and me.

"Yeah!" Mortimer taunted. "You probably took the real egg out of the hole and lugged it back to Harmon's clubhouse. You sure went to a lot of trouble to louse things up!"

48

"Tell it to the Marines!" said Dinky, not knowing what to say.

We stood there with our arms folded, waiting to see what happened next. None of us knew any more about what was going on than Mayor Scragg did. The Mayor was trying desperately to apologize to the professor, but the professor wasn't paying any attention to him. He was standing in the middle of the clearing, chewing on his spectacles and muttering to himself.

"What I don't understand," he kept saying, "is that my friend Dr. Hoffmeister at the museum was so certain those shell fragments came from the Jurassic period. He might be misled by a photograph, but not by the pieces of shell. . . . They were subjected to very scientific tests. . . . I don't understand it. I don't understand it at all."

"Perhaps there never was an egg," suggested a reporter. "Maybe all that the boys found were pieces of shell, and they invented the egg."

"Ah, perhaps so," said the professor. "But then they were extremely clever. Because the weight and the dimensions that they sent to the museum checked exactly with what we would expect for the egg of a brontosaurus."

"Excuse me, Professor!" came a voice from the crowd. "I can show you where the real egg is."

"What's that?"

Harmon Muldoon and Stony Martin pushed their way to the center of the clearing. "We found the real dinosaur egg," said Harmon. "I made up this dummy egg and planted it in the quarry to fool these other guys. It sure worked, too. They've spent about two weeks trying to hatch that hunk of plaster."

"Then I suppose you're the one who made these very authentic-looking footprints in the sand?"

"Yes!" said Harmon. "We figured that would give them a real charge."

"Well, you're a very clever young man," said the professor. "Now, supposing you show us the real egg."

"It's back at our clubhouse," said Harmon, and he started to lead the way back up the path.

"Harmon has always been one of the cleverest young lads in Mammoth Falls," Mayor Scragg confided to the professor, as he hurried to keep up with him over the rough ground. "I'll have to remember to tell him so."

The rest of us fell in behind them, and as we trudged back out to the road the members of the Mad Scientists' Club were the most dejected lot you ever saw. But I noticed that Henry had stayed behind and was searching among the broken chunks of plaster in the sand. I saw him put something in his pocket, and when he caught up with the rest of us he was wearing that quiet, mysterious smile again.

It was pretty hot on the second floor of Stony Martin's garage, and Mayor Scragg was already mopping the top of his head with his handkerchief on the way up the stairs. When Professor Mudgeon saw the big egg on the table he sucked a lot of air in through his teeth and lunged toward it with his hands outstretched.

"Ah, yes! This looks like the real thing," he exclaimed. "And such a beauty, too!"

The reporters were crowding around him as he bent over it with his glass. Somehow or other, Henry had managed to worm his way in among them and was standing right at the professor's shoulder.

"The light isn't very good here, Professor. Why don't we take it over to the window."

"An excellent idea," said the professor, "but be very careful. This looks like a very valuable fossil specimen."

"Oh, I'm sure it is," said Henry, as he spun around with the thing held lightly in his hands.

"Wait a minute! I'll carry it!" said Harmon Muldoon, grabbing Henry by the elbow.

"Look out!" Henry cried. The egg popped out of his hands and crashed to the floor, where it practically exploded into a litter of shards and white powder. "Gosh, I'm sorry, Harmon!" said Henry. "I'll clean it up for you."

"Never mind!" said Harmon, looking aghast at the mess on the floor. "I guess you win, Henry." And he crushed a big chunk of the plaster under the heel of his shoe. Something bright among the powder glinted in the faint light from the window. Harmon bent down and picked it up. "Hey, that's my ring!" he said. "I lost it when I took it off the other day to mix the ——"

"To mix what?" asked Henry.

"Never mind," said Harmon, sheepishly. Then he looked hard at Henry. "Hey! This must be the egg that I cast to put out in the swamp. How did it ever get back in here?"

"I haven't the faintest idea," said Henry.

"But the one out in the swamp ——"

"Was a fake!" said Henry.

"So you were a step ahead of me all the time!"

Professor Mudgeon cleared his throat. "Excuse me! But I'm thoroughly confused."

"You said a mouthful, Professor!" muttered

Dinky, as he stepped up to Henry with his face all red. "Do you mean you had us spend all night carrying chunks of plaster back and forth to that stinkin' swamp?"

"It wasn't my idea for you to switch those eggs," said Henry, calmly.

"Well, that wasn't very scientific," Dinky pouted.

"No!" Henry agreed. "But it was pretty funny."

"Well, you sure had me fooled," Harmon admitted. "I really thought you had found a genuine dinosaur egg out there in the quarry."

"We did!" said Henry.

"You did?"

The reporters pricked up their ears at this, and a barrage of questions hit Henry from all directions. But Mayor Scragg's voice trumpeted over all of them.

"Well, where is it, you young fool — I mean, won't you tell us where it is, Henry?"

"It's out in the swamp," said Henry, wiping the perspiration off his glasses, "but in a different place."

"Oh no! Not out in that swamp again!" groaned the Mayor, looking down at his muddy feet.

"Just a minute. I'm puzzled about one thing," said Mr. Bowden. "My paper will want to know why you buried that fake egg in the first place, and why you led us out there on a wild-goose chase."

"I'm sorry about that," Henry apologized. "But without mentioning any names, I had an idea somebody would try to swipe the real egg. So I made a plaster cast of it the first night we brought it in, and took the real egg right out to the swamp and buried it. I couldn't resist taking you out to where the fake egg was buried, because you never would have gotten the whole story if I hadn't."

"And the culprit never would have come to light," boomed Mayor Scragg, fixing a baleful glare on Harmon Muldoon.

"I think the Professor will agree that a scientist can't be too careful about protecting his discoveries," Henry observed.

It was the professor's turn to wipe off his glasses. "Yes. . . . Hmm. . . . Uh," he stammered. "Unfortunately, history provides us with some classic examples of fraud and deception in the natural sciences — er — particularly in the field of paleontology, I may say."

"Like the Piltdown man?" questioned Mr. Bowden.

As we went down the stairs and out into

Egan's Alley, Mayor Scragg was again hovering at Professor Mudgeon's shoulder. "That young Muldoon lad always was a meddlesome boob!" he said, confidentially.

"Very interesting! Very interesting!" said the professor.

Henry led us this time to the opposite side of the swamp, near where the White Fork road starts up into the hills. Not far off the road, at the foot of a bluff, he stopped at a point in the middle of a white stretch of sand. He dug into the sand with his hands and unearthed the big egg. It looked just the way it had that first night. Dinky carried it over to the professor to examine.

"Now I know why it felt so light that next day," he said.

The professor was enthused, and Mayor Scragg beamed proudly. "Truly a beautiful specimen," said the professor.

"Looks kind of ugly to me," said the Mayor. "But then, you know best, Professor."

While the professor was examining the egg, and everybody with a camera was taking pictures of it, I noticed Henry pulling something else out of the hole in the sand.

"What's that you have there, Henry?" I asked. It looked like one of our miniature transmitters.

"It's a sort of booby trap I rigged up as a burglar alarm," he said, and showed it to me. It was a little transmitter, all right, but Henry had rigged it with a pressure-type switch.

"As long as the egg was sitting on top of it, it kept on sending out a steady signal that I could pick up back at the clubhouse," he explained. "But if anyone moved the egg, the transmitter would shut off, and I'd know something was wrong."

"That was why you were never really worried about the egg?"

"That's right! I knew the real egg was here all the time, safe and sound. Any time I wanted to check, I'd just tune in this beep on our receiver."

Then I looked at him hard.

"Henry," I said, "is that what I saw you putting in your pocket over there when we dug up the fake egg? Is that why you knew we were in Stony Martin's garage that night we switched the eggs?"

"Oh, that?" said Henry. "That was a little different. When I cast the fake egg I did happen to drop one of these transmitters into the plaster. No matter where the egg went I could always follow the beep with our directional antenna. It seemed like a good idea at the time."

"So you tracked us all the way from Stony's garage out to the swamp, and then slipped over there just to scare the life out of us!"

"Not exactly. I wanted to make sure you were all right."

Then another thought struck me. "Come to think of it, Henry, you knew the minute Harmon had swiped that egg, and you also knew where he took it."

"Just about."

"But you let everybody poke fun at Dinky and Freddy for claiming the egg had been stolen!"

"I am a little ashamed of that," Henry admitted. "But I didn't want to louse up my plan. If I had admitted that the egg had been stolen, all you guys would have wanted to raid Harmon's clubhouse, and we wouldn't have had nearly as much fun."

"You mean *you* wouldn't!" I told him, shaking my head.

When the professor had finished examining the big egg he announced he was satisfied that it was genuine. He also asked the Mayor if the museum and the university could have the permission of the town authorities to conduct further excavations in the old quarry, in the hope that further fossil remains might be uncovered. Never one to stand in the way of the forward march of science, or the possible establishment of a tourist attraction, the Mayor assured him that the town would be most cooperative.

"What are you going to do with this egg?" asked one of the reporters.

Professor Mudgeon looked at Mayor Scragg, and Mayor Scragg turned and looked at Henry.

"What *do* you do with a dinosaur egg?" he asked.

"Usually they go into museums," said Henry.

"Unless the International Egg Syndicate happens to get hold of them," said Mortimer Dalrymple, *sotto voce*.

"I'm certain the American Museum of Natural History would be very pleased to have it," said Professor Mudgeon, suggestively.

"I suppose they would," mused Henry. "On the other hand, would you mind if we tried to hatch it first? They might rather have a live brontosaurus."

"Ohhh . . . I'm sure they would," said the professor, amidst the general laughter. Then with a gallant bow he added, "Why don't you proceed with your experiment, Professor Mulligan. The museum and I will be happy to wait our turn."

"After you, Professor!" said Henry Mulligan, indicating the path leading back to the cars.

"After *you*, Professor!" said Professor Mudgeon, waving Henry before him.

While they were gesticulating, Mayor Scragg stepped ahead of both of them and walked grandly up the path, beaming broadly.

We checked on the egg, off and on, for several weeks. Then one day Dinky and Freddy came tearing up the driveway to Jeff's barn on their bicycles.

"The egg has hatched! The egg has hatched!" Dinky was shouting, long before he was in earshot.

"Honest Injun! May my mother have pneumonia if I'm telling a lie!" cried Freddy.

We all got on our bikes and pedaled out the White Forks road as fast as we could.

"See, there!" shouted Dinky, as soon as we had gotten to the stretch of sand by the bluff. He was pointing to a shallow pit where the egg lay, broken into three pieces. Down by the water's edge were the same footprints we had seen before. But this time there was a definite line in the wet sand about as thick as a clothesline, waving among the tracks.

"Look! There's his tail! There's his tail!" Freddy shouted, while he jumped up and down.

We searched the bushes and the shores of the swamp for several hundred yards on either side of the little beach, but we could find no more footprints.

"It couldn't have gone into the water," Dinky blubbered. "Dinosaurs couldn't swim."

"That's right," Henry nodded. "They went into shallow water when they got too heavy to stand upright on dry land. But they were heavy enough to sink, even in loose mud. That's why so many of their skeletons were preserved as fossils."

Henry spent a long time studying the egg fragments and the footprints. Then he professed himself stumped.

"I don't know what to think," he said finally. "I'd like to think that we had hatched a live dinosaur, but if we can't find it we'll never know. It could just as well be that Harmon ended up a step ahead of us this time, after all."

The Secret of
the Old Cannon

We all wondered why Homer Snodgrass had been spending so much time at the library with Daphne Muldoon. We knew he was sweet on her. But what can you do in a library except look at books? Anyway, they'd been there 'most every night until the library closed, and we hadn't seen Homer around the clubhouse for three weeks.

The next time we had a meeting of the Mad Scientists' Club, Jeff Crocker, our president, said that if Homer didn't show up at the next regular meeting we would take a vote on whether we should revoke his membership. We never did take the vote, though. I had just finished reading the minutes of the last meeting when all of a sudden Homer burst through the door of Jeff Crocker's barn.

"I've got something important to bring up before the club," he said, kind of all out of breath.

Jeff Crocker rapped his gavel on the old packing crate we use for the president's podium, and told Homer to sit down.

"We've got to go through the old business yet," he said. "If there's any time left when we get through, you can have first turn, Homer."

Homer slouched back on his stool and pretended to look out of the window as if he wasn't interested in any old business.

Then we had a long discussion about how we might raise some more money, but it was pretty evident that we weren't going to get a hot idea because there wasn't any smoke coming out of anybody's ears.

Finally Homer couldn't stand it any more, and he stood right up and blurted out, "I know where you can get a whole bunch of money! Not just a little bit — a whole bunch!"

Jeff rapped his gavel hard on the packing case and shouted at Homer, "I thought I told you to wait until we got around to new business!"

Homer sat down again, but right away Jeff thought better of it.

"What was that you said about money?"

"I didn't say a thing," said Homer, and he turned around and looked out of the window again.

"I make a motion that Homer Snodgrass tell us what he's thinking about," said little Dinky Poore.

"I second the motion," said pudgy Freddy Muldoon.

Then it took a lot of coaxing to get Homer to stop looking out of the window, and Jeff had to apologize for making him wait so long. Finally Homer stood up.

"Well, Daphne Muldoon had to do this story for the school paper, and she asked me to help her with it," said Homer.

Mortimer Dalrymple began to snicker, and Homer turned around and glared at him, and Jeff had to rap his gavel on the podium again.

"You can laugh if you want to," said Homer, "but I think we found out where there's a whole bunch of money hidden."

"Where?" asked Jeff.

"Inside that old cannon out at Memorial Point," said Homer.

The cannon he was talking about is a big old Civil War monster that sits on the south slope of Brake Hill about five miles outside of Mammoth Falls. It points right down the valley where

Lemon Creek flows toward the river. It was put up there to protect the town from an attack from the South, but as far as anyone knows it never fired a shot. After the war it was just left there because it was too heavy to move. Eventually the town made a little park around it and erected a couple of statues of Civil War soldiers. Nowadays everyone calls the place Memorial Point, and it's a great place for family picnics.

Homer and Daphne had spent many evenings in the library going through old issues of the Mammoth Falls *Gazette* to trace the history of the old cannon. They managed to find out where the gun had been cast, how many horses it took to haul it up the hill where it sits now, how far it could fire a fifteen-inch ball, and all sorts of interesting stuff like that.

After the Civil War there wasn't much written about the cannon. Daphne and Homer went through hundreds of copies of the weekly *Gazette* before they found any mention of it again. Then it cropped up in the news in 1910 when the Town Council voted to have the barrel plugged up with concrete to keep kids from crawling inside it. There was a big hullabaloo in town at the time, because somebody's kid had disappeared and a lot of people thought he had been inside the cannon when they plugged it up. They were just about to chip all the cement out of the barrel when the kid turned up in Cairo, Illinois. Seems he had fallen asleep in a box car down in the railroad yards and got all the way to Cairo before he could get anybody to let him out. Funny thing! His name was Alonzo Scragg, and now he's the mayor of our town.

That was an exciting week for Mammoth Falls. And for the Scragg family, too. Just before young Alonzo disappeared, somebody with a bandanna tied around his nose held up the Mammoth Falls Trust and Deposit Company and got away with $75,000 in cold cash. He rode off on a horse down the Old South Road, and nobody ever saw him or the cash again.

A lot of people thought they recognized the horse, though. They said it looked like one that belonged to Elijah Scragg, Alonzo's grandfather. It was a strawberry roan with a white splash on its nose, and there wasn't another one like it for miles around.

Old Elijah was in high dudgeon, according to the newspaper accounts. He swore up and down that the horse had been missing for two days, and he figured somebody stole it just to pull off the bank job and throw suspicion on him. There was a big investigation and a regular court hearing. Elijah had two of his hired men to back him up on his testimony, but nobody was ever sure whether the three of them weren't in cahoots on the robbery.

Elijah Scragg had been running for his tenth term on the Town Council. The judge ruled that there wasn't enough evidence to bring him to trial; but the mere fact he was suspected of being connected with the bank robbery ruined his chances for election. Emory Sharples, who was running against him, made a lot of the incident, and he got elected in Elijah's place.

The Scraggses and the Sharpleses are two of the oldest families in Mammoth Falls, and they have always been great rivals; but after the bank robbery they were sworn enemies. They carried on a political feud that still goes on today. Whenever a Scragg runs for some town office, the Sharpleses always make sure they have somebody to run against him.

This year was no exception. Mayor Scragg's term of office was due to expire, and Abner Sharples had announced himself a candidate. Abner is a young fellow, but he's one of the smartest lawyers in Mammoth Falls, and everybody figured he might get a few votes if he worked hard.

Daphne and Homer had come up with a theory about the robbery. One witness had seen a rider heading up Brake Hill on the strawberry roan. They figured he must have cut off through the countryside, because he wasn't seen going through any other town. And if Elijah Scragg's horse was returned to his pasture the next morning, he couldn't have gone very far. He must have lived somewhere nearby and he probably would have hidden the money somewhere until the affair blew over. The old Civil War cannon out at Memorial Point seemed like a good hiding place. They got more suspicious about it when they discovered three more stories in the *Gazette* complaining about vandals who kept trying to chip the concrete out of the barrel.

"What makes you think there's any money hidden in the old cannon?" Jeff asked.

"Just a hunch," said Homer. "It seemed like such a coincidence that it got plugged up the same week the bank was robbed."

"You mean you think the bank robber hid the money in the cannon, and then before he could get it out again the Town Council sent a crew out there to plug up the barrel with cement?"

"That's what we figure," said Homer, not so sure of himself now. "The money has never been found. We checked on that with old Mr. Willis down at the bank. Daphne's gonna do a story on the whole thing for the school paper and she figures she's got a real scoop."

"It'd make a better story if somebody could prove the money was really there," Mortimer chipped in.

"Bet that old robber was mad when he got back and found that cannon full of cement," Freddy observed.

"He sure put it in a safe place," said Dinky. "I wonder if it's been earning interest?"

"Just historical interest," quipped Mortimer.

Jeff rapped his gavel on the packing crate again.

"Maybe some of you geniuses can figure out how we're going to find out if the money's there!"

As soon as he said "genius" everybody turned and looked at Henry Mulligan. Henry was just sitting there on the old piano stool, leaning back against the barn wall and staring up at the rafters. There was a reverent silence in the clubhouse. Nobody ever spoke when Henry was doing his thinking.

Finally Henry let his stool come forward again and looked slowly around the clubhouse. "What kind of gun is it?" he asked.

"My old man said it was a Parrott gun," said Freddy.

"It isn't a Parrott gun," Dinky interrupted. "It's a Rodman. I can show you in a book I got at home. It tells all about the Civil War."

"You're nuts," Freddy argued. "My old man ought to know."

"A Parrott gun is a lot different," Dinky persisted. "This one's a Rodman."

"I think I know how we can find out what's in it," Henry said quietly.

Then everybody shut up. Because Henry was looking up at the rafters of Jeff's barn and had tilted his stool back to the thinking position again.

Just then somebody burped. Everybody looked around at Freddy Muldoon. He's the champion burper in the Mad Scientists' Club, and everybody naturally looks at him when someone uncorks one. But this time Freddy was looking around too. His face wore a frown.

"I think that came from outside," he said.

Mortimer and I made a rush for the door. Sure enough, there was Harmon Muldoon, Freddy's sneaky cousin, just disappearing down the alley and rounding the corner into Vesey Street. We went back inside.

"Harmon Muldoon's been spying on us again," said Mortimer.

"I'll bet he heard everything we said," chirped Dinky.

"That means he probably knows all about the old cannon and the money," groaned Homer. "Now it'll be all over town. Harmon's a big blabbermouth."

"We'd better get moving if we're going to do anything," Mortimer urged.

All eyes automatically turned toward Henry Mulligan. Henry was still leaning back against the wall, wiping his horn-rimmed glasses. He stood up and said, "Jeff, I think we'd better go see Dr. Hendricks at the university."

Dr. Paul Hendricks is head of the Medical School of the State University, and one of the best friends of the Mad Scientists' Club. He was the one who helped Henry figure out where to hatch the dinosaur egg last year.

"Are you sick, Henry?" Jeff asked. "How can Dr. Hendricks help us find out what's in that cannon?"

"I'll tell you on the way there," said Henry. "Do you think your mother would drive us over to the university?"

"I'll ask her," said Jeff. "What do you want the other fellows to do?"

"I'd suggest they plan to be at Memorial Point about eight o'clock tonight," said Henry, "just after it gets dark. And let's not have a gang-rush out there! Wander out there one at a time, like nothing special was going on. If anybody sees Harmon Muldoon, lead him off the scent somewhere on a wild-goose chase. The less he knows from here on in, the better."

"O.K., Major Mulligan!" said Dinky Poore, throwing Henry a highball signal.

We met that night at the foot of Brake Hill. Everybody was there early except Henry and Jeff.

"Why do we have to come out here at night?" asked Freddy Muldoon. "It's kind of spooky!"

"Not so loud!" Mortimer cautioned in a whisper. "We don't want anybody to know what we're doing. And besides, we gotta think about Elmer Pridgin. He's always roamin' around these woods with that old squirrel rifle. I heard he takes pot shots at people."

"I don't believe it!" whispered little Dinky. "Elmer's all right. People just don't understand him, that's all."

"He's a little soft in the head, but he wouldn't hurt anybody," said Freddy in a hoarse croak, pushing his pudgy face up close to Mortimer's.

"Oh yeah! How come he never comes into town? And what does he live on, out there in the woods?" Mortimer hissed.

"He does, too, come into town!" Freddy argued, his voice getting a little louder. "He comes in every year to vote on Town Meeting day — and he gets a haircut then, too."

"Glory be!" said Mortimer. "Is that when he buys his groceries?"

"He doesn't need any groceries," Dinky chimed in. "He raises his own vegetables out by his cabin. He can snare rabbits with just a piece of string, and he'll skin one faster than you can tie your shoes. He's smart, Elmer is."

"Very elucidative!" said Mortimer. Mortimer always likes to use big words.

"Jiggers!" Homer warned. "Somebody's coming."

We all dove into the bushes by the side of the road. There were two bicycles coming from the direction of town. Freddy, who's a little slow on his feet, was the last one to get under cover, and when he hit the ground he burped a real loud one.

"Is that you, Freddy?" came Jeff's voice.

"No! It's my uncle," Freddy answered. "We brought him along for laughs."

"All right, let's cut the comedy," Jeff cautioned. "We've got lots of work to do."

Henry and Jeff pulled their bicycles into the

brush and we started up the hill. As usual, Henry had brought along a lot of mysterious-looking apparatus that we all had to carry, and he kept telling us to be careful with it because it was very delicate.

"Has anybody seen Harmon Muldoon?" Jeff inquired.

"No sign of him anywhere," Dinky puffed. "Maybe he gave up the ghost."

"I wouldn't be too sure," Henry observed. "He might be up by the old cannon. Maybe we'd better send scouts up first, and stake out some security, too. What do you think, Jeff?"

Jeff agreed. We all put down our loads, and Mortimer and Homer went on ahead to scout out the area around Memorial Point. They came back in a few minutes and reported everything clear. We went on up the hill then, with all our gear. It was misty that night, and there was a pale moon darting in and out behind the clouds. The little clearing around the old cannon had an eerie air about it. The tablet the town had erected at the mouth of the clearing, and the statues of the Confederate and Union soldiers, cast long shadows on the sloping hillside. The monstrous gun itself looked like some fat-bellied, prehistoric reptile, squatting on its haunches in the shadow of the trees, waiting to devour any unsuspecting victim that wandered within its reach. In the misty moonlight, the thing looked three times as big as it ever had before.

"Gosh! I wonder what this thing weighs?" Mortimer gulped.

"The barrel alone weighs forty-nine thousand pounds," Homer explained, "but they made some that weighed twice as much as this one." All of a sudden Homer had become a real expert in such matters.

Jeff sent Mortimer and Dinky out to stand security guard at points where they could watch the approaches to the clearing from the road and from the path that wound along the ridge of Brake Hill. They were to give the hoot-owl signal if they saw anyone coming. The rest of us got to work setting up Henry's infernal apparatus.

Henry clambered up on top of the cannon, near the rear, where it bellied out into a huge bottle-shaped bulge about four feet thick. He felt along the top of it with his fingers until he located the breech vent hole. Then he pulled a pencil flashlight out of his pocket and peered down into the hole, cupping his hand around it so the light wouldn't show.

"What's he doin'?" croaked Freddy. "He can't

see through that hunk of iron with that thing, can he?"

"He's looking down the breech vent," Homer explained in a whisper. "That's the hole they used to stick the primer in to ignite the powder charge, but it's probably all rusty and clogged up now."

Henry stuck his left hand out. "Rod!" he ordered. I handed him the gun-cleaning rod we'd brought along. He rammed it up and down inside the hole a few times, but it didn't go down very far. Henry handed it back. "Drill! Three-eighths bit with extension." I stuck a bit in the battery-operated drill he had and handed it to him. Henry wrapped it in a burlap bag to muffle the noise and inserted the long, slender extension in the hole. In a few seconds he broke through the obstruction that had stopped him and asked for the rod again. He pumped it up and down until its full length disappeared down the hole. Henry pulled it out, and his left hand flashed out again.

"Hand me that long case," he said. "And be very careful with it."

I handed him a long black case that was among the paraphernalia he and Jeff had brought. It looked like something you might keep a three-hundred-dollar fishing rod in. Henry laid it on top of the cannon and opened it. From it, he drew a long, squirmy-looking thing that glinted in the moonlight. It bent in his hands as he carefully inserted the end of it into the breech vent and fed it down the hole until he came to the place he'd marked with a piece of tape.

"Clamp!" hissed Henry.

"Clamp!" I hissed back, handing him a felt-lined gadget from among the assortment of instruments he had laid out on a pad. Henry pinched the clamp into place so it held the log, flexible tube suspended in the vent hole just where he wanted it. Then he stopped to mop his brow.

"Anyone coming?" he asked.

"No!" I answered. "Jeff'll let us know. Let's get on with it, Henry."

Henry mopped his brow again and went on with the operation. I kept handing things up to him, and I could see Henry was getting more and more excited as he fitted each piece of apparatus to the Rube Goldberg contraption he was creating on top of the cannon. The long tube he had stuck down the vent hole had two strands to it. Each of them was wrapped in some kind of insulation and had a finely threaded fitting on the end. Henry separated the two strands and screwed a shiny metal cylinder onto one of them. He had me connect a wire lead to it from a dry cell. Then he asked for the large black box that was sitting on the pad, and he pulled what looked like a very fancy camera out of it. He screwed the threaded end of the other strand into the face of it. Then he pulled the pencil flashlight out of his pocket and started checking all the settings. Finally he asked for the other wire lead from the batteries, and hooked it to a terminal on the camera.

Freddy Muldoon, who had clambered up onto the gun carriage to peer at what Henry was doing, could no longer restrain his curiosity. "What's that crazy contraption, Henry? You gonna blow the whole cannon to smithereens?"

Henry was so excited I could see his hands were trembling, and he was exasperated by Freddy's question. But he answered it patiently enough.

"This is what you call a gastroscope," he explained. "Doctors use it to take pictures inside people's stomachs. Now if you'll keep your fat face shut, we might get a few good pictures of the inside of this cannon!"

Freddy grunted and slid down off the carriage, muttering something about cranky geniuses.

Henry took four shots with the camera. After each shot he would adjust the length of the flexible tube where the clamp held it at the top of the vent hole, so he could get pictures from different depths inside the cannon's breech. Each time he took a shot you could see a little flash of light escape from the breech vent.

"How does this thing work?" I asked in a whisper.

"It's really quite simple," said Henry. "This metal cylinder, here, is just a small strobe light. The tube sticking down the hole consists of two optical fibers, insulated from each other. One of them carries the light down to illuminate the interior of the cavity you're photographing. The other one has a small lens on the end of it, and it carries the reflected light back up to the camera. The camera aperture is the same diameter as the glass fiber, and the lens is a regular camera lens. It magnifies the image that the optical fiber sends up, and you have a regular photograph."

"Gee whizz!" I said.

"We'll soon know if there's anything inside there —" Henry said, "providing everything worked all right!"

Just then somebody burped again — a real rumbler. Jeff Crocker stepped out of the shadow of the trees at the edge of the clearing, where he had been standing guard, and walked over to Freddy Muldoon.

"Listen, Freddy," Jeff warned, "Stop that! One

more of those and we're going to leave you back at the clubhouse after this."

"That wasn't me!" Freddy insisted. "Honest, Jeff, I didn't even open my mouth."

Jeff swung around in our direction. "Well, who was it then?" he demanded.

"I think it came from over there," said Freddy, pointing in the direction of the east side of the clearing, where the statue of the Confederate soldier stood.

Jeff dashed to that side of the clearing and poked around among the bushes. Then he came back to where we were standing by the cannon. "I've got a feeling there's somebody around here who isn't supposed to be," he said. Then he turned back toward the trees where he had been standing guard. "Wait a minute! I've got an idea."

There was a caretaker's toolshed a few feet back in the woods, and we could hear the door of it creak as Jeff opened it. In a minute he was back in the clearing, trailing a long length of garden hose behind him. "Go back in the shed and turn the water on full!" he whispered to Homer.

The next thing we knew, a high-pressure stream of water shot out of the end of the hose. To our amazement, Jeff directed it straight at the statue of the Confederate soldier. The full force of the stream hit the statue square in the side of the face. The Rebel cap flew off its head and landed in the bushes at the edge of the clearing. The statue lost its balance and toppled to the ground.

What happened next we couldn't believe. No sooner had the statue hit the ground than it bounced to its feet, let out a Rebel yell, and hightailed it down the hill toward the road. By the time we came to our senses, it had disappeared in the dense undergrowth of the lower slope.

Jeff was laughing so hard he dropped the hose and rolled on the ground. We all got a good soaking before Homer could dash back to the shed and shut off the water.

"That guy can run as fast as my cousin Harmon," said Freddy Muldoon.

"That *was* your cousin Harmon!" Jeff blurted out from where he was sitting on the ground. "He's been waiting here for us ever since it got dark."

"How'd you know he was there?" I asked.

"I stumbled over the real statue when I went back in the bushes over there," Jeff explained. "I knew there were only two statues up here, so one of the Rebels had to be a fake!"

"Pretty sneaky!" said Freddy Muldoon.

"Reminds me of 'The Purloined Letter,'" Henry observed. "Here we are, with scouts staked out for security, looking under rocks and bushes for snoopers, and Harmon was standing right in the middle of us all the time. I always did say Harmon was smart. You've got to give him credit."

"Yeah! And that means he heard everything we said and knows everything we did," said Homer.

"Except," said Henry, tapping his camera, "he doesn't know what we have on this film!"

Before we left Memorial Point, Henry put us all to work rigging up some more of his infernal apparatus. From his duffel bag he took two round objects about the size of overcoat buttons and taped them to the underside of the cannon, where they couldn't be seen.

"What are these things, Henry?" asked Freddy.

"They're silicon infrared detectors," said Henry. "They're very sensitive to small changes in temperature. If anybody comes near the cannon, the heat of his body will be enough to set up a small electric current in them. We can use that current to trigger a circuit and start a radiosonde beacon sending out a signal. If we keep a receiver turned on back at the clubhouse, we can record that signal on a graph. If anybody comes nosing around here, we'll know when he came and how long he stayed."

"How'll we know who it is?" asked Dinky.

"I brought along some infrared film," Henry explained. "We can rig up a camera in the same circuit and get a pretty good picture even in the dark — probably good enough so we can recognize who was here."

"Jeepers!" said Freddy. "You scientists think of everything."

We wired the circuit so the radio beacon and the camera were hidden in a tree back of the cannon, and went back to the clubhouse.

Mortimer developed the pictures Henry had taken as soon as we got back to our lab. We all crowded around Henry as he peered at the negatives over a light box. The first two didn't seem to have anything at all on them. But the third negative showed something leaning against the wall of the cannon's chamber that looked like the leather handle on an old satchel.

"We'll have to enlarge this one and get a good, clear print," Henry said. "I think I see something interesting here."

Mortimer stuck the negative in the enlarger and turned out all the lights in the lab. He blew it up as big as he could, and we all held our breath as he brought it into focus. When he got it good and sharp, we could all see what Henry was talking about. The outline of the handle was very clear, and right beneath it, on the top of the satchel, was a metal nameplate. You could make out the initials easily. They were EMS.

The next morning we were all at the clubhouse early for a strategy meeting. Mortimer was over in the corner where we have all our ham radio gear set up, checking the ink trace on the oscillograph we had hooked up to our receiver. He pointed to a place where the needle had made a jagged line on the graph paper. "Someone was out there by the cannon about midnight," he said excitedly.

"I'll bet Harmon went back out there after we left," said Jeff.

"Let's go out there and see if we got a picture of him," said Henry. "Maybe we can tell who it was."

Just then the needle on the recorder started to jiggle again. We all looked at it for a minute, and it gave me a funny feeling. There was somebody up by the cannon, thinking he was all alone, and here we were, about five miles away, practically watching his every move on a piece of paper.

Mortimer turned up the volume on the receiver. We could hear the *beep, beep, beep* of the radio beacon every time the visitor moved near the cannon.

"Let's get out there!" said Homer. "We ought to find out who it is."

"Maybe we should have bugged it with a microphone," Mortimer declared, "so we could listen in on what they're saying."

"Maybe it's just a couple of old cows having a bull session," said Dinky to Freddy Muldoon.

"That's all right," observed Freddy, with the back of his hand to his face. "Mortimer digs that stuff. He could understand what they're saying!"

It was still early morning when we got out to Memorial Point and hid our bicycles in the brush. We split up into two groups for the climb up the hill, so we could approach the clearing from both sides.

Jeff and Henry and I were just about a hundred yards from the clearing when he heard the thump of a rifle shot and the twang of a bullet ricocheting off metal. We froze in our tracks, not daring to move or breathe. Finally Henry whispered, "That sounded like a big-bore rifle."

84

We fell flat on our stomachs in the brush as two wild-eyed figures came dashing pell-mell down the path from the clearing. In the lead by a good margin was Harmon Muldoon, using his best running form. Thumping behind him came the ponderous form of Abner Sharples, his tie fluttering wildly in the breeze and his hat clapped to the back of his head by a pudgy hand. They passed within three feet of us, but they were so intent on getting down off Brake Hill in record time that they didn't even see us. Harmon was right out of sight in no time, and the last we saw of Abner Sharples was his coattail flying through the air as his feet went out from under him on a sharp turn, and he went rolling down the hill like a barrel of lard. His hat flew off his head and landed on a bush.

"I'll bet he beats Harmon to the bottom," said Henry, as he scrambled over to retrieve the hat.

"He sure took a short cut," Jeff snickered. "I wonder what Abner was doing up here?"

"I imagine Harmon has told him everything, and he's hoping to find some evidence connecting Mayor Scragg with the stolen money," said Henry.

"They've got to get it out of the cannon first," Jeff answered. "Let's see if we can find out what happened up there."

We crept forward through the brush, trying to be as quiet as possible. When we got up close to the clearing we stopped and peered out through the bushes. A tall, gaunt man was standing beside the cannon, shading his eyes from the morning sun as he looked down the hill toward the road. A long and ancient-looking squirrel rifle was grasped in his right hand.

"Elmer Pridgin!" Jeff whispered. "He must have fired that shot."

"I guess Mortimer was right," I said. "I wonder why he's so cranky about that old cannon?"

"I don't know, but I think we'd better clear out of here," Jeff hissed back. "He must be the one that was out here at midnight."

We skirted the clearing, picked up the other guys, and beat it back to town. "I think things are going to pop wide open now," Henry told us as we pedaled along the Old South Road. "We've got to work fast."

Henry was right. Daphne Muldoon was waiting for us at the clubhouse when we got back. She'd been looking all over town for Homer, and her pretty face was all screwed up into a worried frown.

"Abner Sharples knows all about the old cannon and the money," she complained. "He's going to tell it all to the newspaper, and there goes my story!"

"You can thank your blabbermouth brother for that," said Freddy Muldoon.

"He doesn't know everything," Homer put in. "I bet he'd like to see this picture," and he waved a copy of the photograph of the inside of the cannon in front of Daphne's face.

"Maybe it would be a good idea if he did!" came a voice from the corner.

We all turned around to look at Henry, who was leaning back on his piano stool, looking up at the rafters again. There was a look of evil genius on his face.

Two hours later, Daphne and Homer just happened to be among the tiny knot of curious spectators gathered outside the door of the Town Council meeting room when Abner Sharples appeared to urge the Council to investigate the mystery of the old cannon. Homer just happened to drop the photograph out of the folder he was carrying, and out of the corner of his eye he saw Harmon Muldoon pounce upon it and scoop it up. A moment later he was in excited consultation with Abner Sharples in a corner of the room.

When Homer took off to join the rest of us, Abner Sharples, sweating and puffing, was in the

midst of one of his spellbinding political ha-
rangues. He was waving the photograph in the
faces of the Council, and claiming it represented
clinching evidence that the grandfather of Alonzo
Scraggs had been implicated in the unsolved bank
robbery.

Meanwhile the rest of us were bouncing along
through the dust and ruts of Turkey Run Road in
Zeke Boniface's decrepit old junk truck. Turkey
Run Road winds around behind Brake Hill, and
Henry figured we'd attract less attention if we
went that way. Zeke sat at the wheel of Richard
the Deep Breather and wrestled it manfully
around the curves of the winding road. The
crunched black derby that he always wore over
the bald spot on his head bounced up and down,
and the ashes from his cigar dropped unheeded
onto the front of his grease-stained undershirt.
We always admired the way Zeke could shift that
cigar from one side of his mouth to the other
without using any hands.

Henry and Jeff had decided to take Zeke into
our confidence. We needed some heavy equipment for the job Henry had in mind, and Zeke
always had plenty of block-and-tackle kicking
around his junk yard, as well as an overhead
crane for lifting engines out of junk cars. Besides,

Zeke has a strong back and always keeps his mouth shut.

Zeke brought Richard the Deep Breather to a puffing halt on a signal from Jeff, and Dinky Poore and Freddy Muldoon scrambled off the tailgate. Jeff gave them some last-minute instructions and then sent them scampering off through the woods to find Elmer Pridgin. Their job was to keep Elmer busy showing them how to skin rabbits, so he wouldn't be around taking pot shots at us while we were up at Memorial Point.

"You'll have to keep him busy for two or three hours," Jeff told them, "so make like you're real dumb and can't understand how he skins these rabbits so fast."

"Just act natural and you'll be all right!" Mortimer shouted after them as they disappeared into the edge of the woods.

The rest of us stayed on the truck until Zeke brought it to another sputtering stop at the crest of a little knoll deep in the woods on the back side of Brake Hill. The dirt trail that Zeke had followed off of Turkey Run Road brought us a lot closer to Memorial Point than the Old South Road on the other side of the hill, and we had only about a hundred feet to climb to where the cannon sat. But it took us two trips to lug all our equipment up there. This was when we were glad we had Zeke with us. He was strong as a bear. He could stand two railroad ties upright, throw a carrying strap around them, and tote 'em for ten miles balanced on his back. If he didn't have a strap, he'd use the dirty white galluses he always wore over his woolen undershirt.

On our second trip down to where the truck was parked, Homer came riding up on his bicycle and told us what was going on at the Town Hall. "I think Abner Sharples will talk the Council into having the cement plug chipped out of the cannon barrel," he said. "They seemed to be pretty interested in his story."

"That's great!" said Henry. "Just what we want."

"I doubt if they can get a crew up here before tomorrow," said Jeff, "but we'd better hurry, just the same. Give us a hand with the rest of this stuff, Homer."

We struggled up the hill with all the parts to Zeke's overhead crane and assembled the stanchion at the mouth of the old cannon. Then we all took our hatchets and scoured the woods for good, hard ash that would make a hot fire and not too much smoke. Meanwhile, Zeke drilled a couple of diagonal holes in the end of the cement plug, and fashioned an iron clamp that would bite

90

into the holes like a pair of ice tongs. He hooked one end of a set of block-and-tackle to the clamp and lashed the other end to a tree.

Getting the cement plug out of the barrel was easy, since we were able to use Henry's brains. We built a big bonfire under the cannon, and Mortimer and Jeff heated up the muzzle end with blowtorches. Henry sat on a rock off to the side, making calculations on a pad of notepaper and keeping one eye on a battery of voltmeters he had set up on the ground beside him. The voltmeters were wired to thermocouples Henry had placed at various points along the huge barrel with asbestos tape. This way he could get a picture of the distribution of heat along with barrel and calculate how much it was expanding. From time to time he would give Jeff and Mortimer directions about where to aim the blowtorches.

"I think we're ready," he said, finally. "Give her a slow, easy tug, Zeke!"

Zeke coiled the free end of the rope around one hamlike wrist, dug his left heel into the earth, and gave a long grunt. You could see the muscles bulge through the back of his undershirt as he heaved on the rope. There was a creaking and grinding noise, and the plug started to inch slowly out of the cannon mouth.

Everybody started to cheer and shout advice

and encouragement to Zeke at the same time. He coiled more of the rope around his arm, set his feet again, and bent his back to the task once more. He chomped down on his cigar so hard that he bit clear through it, and the stub end fell on the grass beside him. But a good six inches of the plug was now showing out of the mouth of the cannon.

"Put more wood on that fire," said Henry. "And keep those torches going. That barrel will cool fast, once the air gets in there."

Homer and I piled more branches on and fanned up the blaze. Then we ran to the front of the cannon to adjust the slings on Zeke's hoisting crane. We wheeled the stanchion right over the cannon until we could slip the sling of the front pulley under the exposed end of the cement plug. Then, as Zeke strained on the block-and-tackle, we eased the stanchion forward with each pull, keeping the tension on the front pulley adjusted so the plug could ride free. It wasn't long before we could cinch up the rear sling under the plug, and then we practically walked it the rest of the way out of the barrel.

Zeke Boniface trudged up and stuck his head into the mouth of the cannon. "Watch out!" cried Henry. "That barrel's hot enough to fry you."

We kicked out the bonfire and raked dirt over the embers. Jeff ran up with the hose from the toolshed, and we sprayed water on the barrel until we figured it was cool enough to take a look inside.

Jeff handed Homer a flashlight. "We'll boost you up through the mouth, Homer. You snake inside and see what you find in the breech."

"I wish Dinky was here," said Homer. "This is his type of work."

"You scared?" asked Mortimer.

"How do I know what's in there?" Homer said. "I might run into an old body or something."

"You'll scare him more than he'll scare you, with that skinny frame of yours!" said Mortimer, as he grabbed Homer around the legs.

We all helped stuff Homer into the cannon, and he wiggled out of sight down the black bore. This was a fifteen-inch Rodman, so there was plenty of room for Homer. He could almost crawl on his hands and knees. We could hear him scraping his way along the barrel, and his voice boomed out with a hollow, echoing sound whenever he shouted something back to us. When he got all the way back to the breech he shouted like a maniac.

"I got the bag! But pull me out before I suffocate. It's hot as blazes in here!"

The sound of his voice boomed all the way down the valley, and we could hear it echo back from the hills across Strawberry Lake. Jeff and Mortimer pulled on the rope we had tied to one of Homer's feet and helped him shinny backward out of the bore. He was dirty and sweaty, but he was clutching the handle of a mildewed leather satchel that looked as if it was about to fall apart.

"Was there anything else back there?" asked Henry.

"Yes!" said Homer, rubbing his eyes and spitting through his teeth. "About a dozen old squirrels' nests and two thousand spiders."

We tried to open the leather satchel, but it was locked. Henry turned to Zeke Boniface, who was leaning against the barrel of the Rodman, choosing a fresh cigar butt from an assortment he had wrapped in a piece of cloth.

"You can open this, can't you, Zeke?"

Zeke looked a little offended, but he shuffled over to where we were squatting around the bag and probed with his fingers through the thick, matted hair over his right ear. From it he drew a sharp, pointed instrument about the size of a hairpin, with a right-angled hook on the end of it.

He bent over the satchel and examined the small lock. Then he inserted the hook, and with two deft movements of his fingers the lock snapped open.

Henry pried the moldy bag open and dumped the contents on the ground. We all stood there goggle-eyed. On the grass at our feet lay about two dozen packages of bank notes and a heap of loose bills.

"That isn't real money," said Homer. "It's stage money. Look how big it is."

"It's real money, all right," Henry said quietly. "Bills used to be that size, years ago."

"Let's count it in a hurry and get out of here," said Jeff.

We all pitched in and counted the money. It came to a little over $75,000.

"That's the bank money, all right," said Homer. "That's just what Mr. Willis said was stolen!"

"What do we do now?" asked Mortimer. "Catch a boat for Brazil?"

"We've got a lot to do," Henry answered. "Now's when the fun begins." He dove into his huge duffel bag that seemed to contain one of everything on earth, and emerged with another dusty brown satchel that looked very much like the one at our feet. "I just happened to find this up in our attic," he explained, as he threw it into the mouth of the cannon. We could hear it slide all the way to the back and thud against the rear wall of the breech. Obviously, Henry had some nefarious scheme up his sleeve.

We had to heat up the cannon again in order to ease the cement plug back into the barrel. When we had finished, and cleaned up all the evidence of the bonfire, the giant gun looked as though it hadn't been touched. We trundled Zeke's hoisting crane and all our gear back down the hill to where the truck was parked.

It was a good thing we cleared out when we did. When Zeke had finally maneuvered Richard the Deep Breather back into town, we discovered that a crew from the town road department was already on its way out to Memorial Point to try and unplug the Rodman cannon.

"We should have guessed they'd get moving fast," said Jeff. "Tomorrow's election day, and if Abner Sharples is going to make a big issue out of the bank robbery, he'll have to do it today."

Mortimer and I were detailed to follow the crowd of curious onlookers back to Memorial Point. We didn't want to miss any detail of the maneuverings of Abner Sharples. Henry, Jeff,

96

and Homer went straight to the bank to see Mr. Willis. For the moment we had forgotten all about Dinky and Freddy.

The scene at Memorial Point was full of laughs for us. Mortimer and I sat on a low branch of a tree where we could see everything that was going on, and snickered behind our hands as the town road crew sweated and labored over the job of getting the cement out of the cannon's bore. They had dragged a gasoline-powered air compressor up the hill, and with two jack hammers they took turns chipping away at the concrete. The farther in they got, the tougher the job became, and they had to stop once and send back to town for breathing masks. The silica dust was so bad they could work only a few minutes at a time, and it took hours to drill through to the breech.

Jim Callahan, the city engineer, was in charge of the project, but Abner Sharples kept running around giving orders and making speeches to the crowd so nobody would forget whose idea it was. Harmon Muldoon kept getting in the way trying to hand tools to the men and give them advice so everybody would think he was essential to the operation. Mortimer and I sat up in the tree trying to keep from laughing so we wouldn't attract attention. My side was aching from Mortimer elbowing me in the ribs every time Abner Sharples said something stupid.

It was late in the afternoon when the workers finally chipped through the last bit of cement. Harmon Muldoon got stuffed into the barrel to see what was inside, just because he happened to be hanging around. When he crawled back out, clutching the leather satchel in one hand, the crowd had pressed up close to the cannon's mouth. Abner Sharples grabbed the satchel and held it aloft for everyone to see. Then he gave the shortest political speech on record in Mammoth Falls.

"Follow me!" he said.

Harmon Muldoon turned around with a look of triumph in his eyes, and thumbed his nose at Mortimer and me. We just sat there on the tree limb and stared right through him as if he wasn't even there.

The crowd followed Abner Sharples down the hill to the road, and Mortimer and I tagged along. Abner led the caravan of vehicles back to Mammoth Falls, standing in the back seat of his convertible, waving the brown leather satchel over his head.

A few minutes later he was waving it in front of the Town Council, with most of the spectators from Memorial Point crammed into the meeting room.

"Gentlemen," said Abner, "with the help of the detective work of our young friend Harmon Muldoon here, I think we may have discovered important evidence which will solve the mystery of the 1910 bank robbery."

Harmon Muldoon had a smirk on his face like a Cheshire cat.

"First, I would like to call your attention to the initials on the nameplate of this satchel."

Abner Sharples looked down. Then he looked up at the Council. Then he looked down again. He turned the satchel around. There were no initials. There wasn't even a nameplate. Abner's face fell. He looked toward Harmon, who made a helpless gesture with his hands.

"I could have sworn there were some initials on this bag," said Abner. "However, there doesn't seem to be now. But what is important is what's inside it!" Whipping a penknife out of his pocket he snapped the lock off the rotten leather. With a dramatic movement he upened the satchel and dumped its contents onto the council table. Hundreds of red, white, and blue campaign buttons cascaded from the satchel and clattered onto the table top. A roar of laughter shook the room. Abner Sharples' chin shook with rage as he picked up one of the buttons and read, "Scragg for Mayor."

Mayor Scragg's eyes were popping out of his head as he reached out from the head of the council table and fingered one of the buttons.

"How on earth did these get inside a bag that has been hidden for years in that old cannon?" he asked.

"I suspect that some nefarious schemer got there before me, and is trying to make a laughing-stock of this august Council," said Abner Sharples, in his best oratorical style. He was purple with rage.

"Appears to me the joke's on you, Abner," said Mr. Snodgrass.

Mr. Willis, the president of the bank, rose from his place at the council table. "Gentlemen, if you will permit me, I believe I can clear this matter up," he said. "A few hours ago I had a visit from young Henry Mulligan and two other members of a group of young men who call themselves the Mad Scientists of Mammoth Falls. I believe you are all familiar with the group and with some of the, er — let us say — some of the exploits they have been connected with. In this case, however, I believe they have done the town a service."

Mr. Willis reached under the council table and produced the original brown satchel.

"I believe this may be the bag you were hoping to find in the old cannon," he said, as he placed it on the table. "Henry Mulligan brought it to me late this morning. I am told that it contains the seventy-five thousand dollars that has been missing from the bank for fifty years. I have not opened it myself, since I do not have the key. I think it is best if we open it here in the presence of the Council, so there can be no misunderstanding as to its contents."

Abner Sharples grabbed the bag. "This is the satchel I was speaking of," He said, excitedly. "You can see the initials EMS on the nameplate. . . . I wonder! Could those be the initials of our illustrious townsman Elijah Scragg? Could this bag have been his property? Is it possible that after fifty years this inoffensive little satchel should come back to haunt his descendants and throw a cloud upon his memory?"

Mayor Scragg had turned scarlet, and was gripping the edge of the council table so hard you could hear his knuckles crack.

"Seems to me they could also be the initials of Emory Sharples," said Mr. Snodgrass placidly.

Just then there was a commotion at the door of the council room. Dinky Poore and Freddy

Muldoon were elbowing their way through the crowd. Behind them loomed the spare and weathered figure of Elmer Pridgin. He wore a tattered hunter's cap, and his long squirrel rifle was clutched in a strong right hand.

Dinky squeezed through the press of spectators to Jeff Crocker's side and whispered in his ear. Jeff reached out and plucked the sleeve of Mr. Willis, and the banker bent down to consult with the new arrivals. Abner Sharples started complaining loudly about the interruption. Mayor Scragg, still flushed, pounded his gavel on the table for quiet.

Finally Mr. Willis came forward to the council table once more. "Gentlemen," he said, "I believe we have some important evidence here. I think you all know Elmer Pridgin. He has a story to tell. But since he has had little experience in public speaking, he has asked me to tell it for him."

Mr. Willis turned the motioned Elmer toward the table. Holding the old leather satchel aloft, he asked, "Elmer, have you ever seen this satchel before?"

Elmer shook his head.

"Of course you haven't," Mr. Willis continued, "It was put into that old cannon by someone before you were born." Mr. Willis pointed to Elmer's throat, where a thin, gold chain was visible among the profusion of hair protruding from his shirt collar. "What is that you are wearing around your neck?"

"This here's a key," grunted Elmer, as he slipped the chain over his head.

"May I have it?" Mr. Willis took the chain and passed it among the council members. "You will note, gentlemen, that the small gold key on that chain bears the initials EMS engraved in the same style as those on the nameplate of this satchel." He turned to Elmer again. "What was your mother's name, Elmer?"

" 'Lisbeth!" said Elmer.

"You mean Elizabeth, don't you?"

"I guess so," said Elmer.

"Gentlemen," said Mr. Willis, "those of us old enough to remember know that Jacob Pridgin married a young woman named Elizabeth Margaret Sargent, a member of the old Sargent family over at Hooker's Point. She died, unfortunately, when Elmer was born." Mr. Willis turned to Elmer again. "What did your father tell you to do with this key, Elmer?" he asked.

"He told me to always keep it," answered Elmer. "Someday it might bring me a whole lotta money. He told me to always watch the old cannon out by the point. 'Always watch the cannon,' he said."

"Why did he want you to watch the cannon?"

"I dunno. He just didn't want people messin' around it."

"Gentlemen," said Mr. Willis, addressing the Council once more, "I believe the true story of the bank robbery of 1910, and the secret of the old cannon out at Memorial Point, is plain enough to anyone who wants a piece together the facts. Here is an obviously ancient satchel bearing the initials EMS, which Henry Mulligan and his friends will testify was found in the breech of the cannon. How they got it out of there I don't know, but I expect they will be willing to tell us if it doesn't involve divulging any of their trade secrets.

"Here is a key bearing the same initials in the same style of engraving. It has been in the possession of Elmer Pridgin since his father's death many years ago."

Mr. Willis handed the key back to Elmer. "Elmer," he said, "I would like you to see if that key will open the satchel."

"Just a minute!" cried Abner Sharples, leaping to his feet.

"Why don't you sit down, Abner!" said Mr. Snodgrass, clapping him on the back and forcing him into a chair.

Elmer Pridgin rubbed his thumb over the key and looked warily around the room. Then he set his squirrel rifle carefully on the table and fitted the key into the lock. The satchel popped open. There was a gasp from the roomful of spectators as Mr. Willis dumped its contents on the table and held up two of the bundles of bank notes for examination.

"Obviously, this is the money taken from the bank," he said, riffling through the old bills. "And obviously, Jacob Pridgin knew its whereabouts and had possession of the key to the satchel. Gentlemen, it must be presumed that it was he who held up the bank and used Elijah Scragg's strawberry roan to make his getaway."

Abner Sharples, seething with rage, rose abruptly from his chair and pushed his way through the crowd to the door. A wave of laughter wafted him from the room. Pinned to the back of his coat was one of the red, white, and blue buttons proclaiming "Scragg for Mayor." Anyone watching Mr. Snodgrass at the moment would have seen him snickering quietly to himself.

"Did my daddy do something bad?" asked Elmer, when the room had quieted down.

"I'm afraid he did, Elmer," said Mayor Scragg, still beaming. "But it all happened before you were born. The money has been restored now, and the fault is not yours. We are grateful to you for coming here today to tell us your story."

"It was them kids made me do it," Elmer declared, pointing at Dinky Poore and Freddy Muldoon. "That little freckled one there saw the key fall out of my shirt when I bent over to get a rabbit out of a snare. An' he wouldn't leave off till I told him the whole story. That one's the most curious kid I ever did see!"

"There remains one matter to be cleared up," Mr. Willis interrupted, clearing his throat. "Miss Daphne Muldoon has reminded me that at the time of the robbery the bank had advertised a reward of five thousand dollars in the Mammoth Falls *Gazette*. I believe the directors of the bank will sustain me in the opinion that the offer still stands."

When Mr. Willis said this, all the spectators started to clap their hands and shout, "Hear! Hear!" Mr. Willis held up his hand for silence.

"I just want to announce," he said, "that the members of the Mad Scientists' Club and Miss

Daphne Muldoon are the logical recipients of this reward. I have discussed it with them, and they have asked that half the reward money be given to the university's medical school, and the other half to Elmer Pridgen. I don't know what the medical school had to do with this matter, but I am sure the directors of the bank will have no objection."

It was several days later that we all hiked out to Elmer Pridgin's cabin, where Mr. Willis and Mayor Scragg presented him with his share of the reward money. Henry wanted Elmer to have the infrared photograph our camera had made of him the night we bugged the cannon with detectors. Elmer looked at the photo and scratched his head.

"I don't never go out there after dark, because it's too sceery," he said. "But that sure is a durned good likeness of my daddy, and I do thank ya' fur it!"

Not so many people have picnics at Memorial Point any more.

The Unidentified Flying Man
of Mammoth Falls

Dinky Poore and Freddy Muldoon found the mannequin in the city dump. Some department store had thrown it away because its face was chipped in one little place. But it was handsome, like all window dummies. Little Dinky and pudgy Fred dragged it all the way to Jeff Crocker's barn and set it up in a corner of our laboratory.

Henry Mulligan didn't like this at all. He said we shouldn't be cluttering up the clubhouse with a lot of junk. But when we put the matter to a vote, Henry lost out. Homer Snodgrass, who is almost as brilliant as Henry and Jeff, pointed out that we could make good use of the mannequin for anatomy lessons and recommended we add this subject to our training program.

Freddy Muldoon and Mortimer Dalrymple were appointed a committe of two to paint the human circulatory system on the dummy's front; but they never got around to it. The thing just stood there in the corner for months until everybody got sick of looking at it. Finally Mortimer pulled an old nylon stocking over its head and dubbed it the Invisible Man. The name seemed like a good one, and that's what we always called it — until Henry got his brilliant idea.

We all arrived at the clubhouse one day to find Henry sitting in a chair in the middle of the floor, staring at the mannequin as if he had never seen it before. He stared at it for a long time. Then he pushed his horn-rimmed glasses up onto his forehead and stared up at the ceiling of the lab.

There was the usual reverent silence. Henry always claimed that when he tilted his head back it made the blood flow to the back of his brain, which was where he kept his best ideas. Then he'd tilt his head forward again and a good idea would pop out.

It worked this time, all right. What came out of Henry, when he finally brought his eyes down from the ceiling, was probably the zaniest idea he has ever had.

"I think we could make this thing fly," said Henry.

"Holy smokes!" said Dinky Poore. "Are you some kind of a nut or something? Don't answer that."

"It's perfectly simple," said Henry, wiping his glasses. "I think we can make the Invisible Man fly, and create a real sensation if we do it right."

"We won't be able to call him the Invisible Man any more," chirped Mortimer. "Maybe we could call him the Flying Sorcerer!"

"Maybe the Air Force would give him an Air Medal. Then he'd have something to wear!" said Freddy.

"That's enough jokes!" Jeff Crocker interrupted.

"Next week is Founders Day," Henry continued. "There's going to be a lot of speeches in the Town Square, and a pageant, and all that stuff. I think we can put on a demonstration with our friend the dummy that'll steal the show. . . . Now, you know where the monument to Hannah Kimball is?"

Hannah Kimball is the heroine of Mammoth Falls. Some people say she founded the town.

Anyway, she was an early settler who defended her cabin against a whole tribe of Indians with just a blunderbuss and a scarecrow. She stuck the scarecrow up through the chimney with a pole. It kept waving its arms even after it had been shot full of Indian arrows, and the attackers got scared and ran away.

After Henry finished outlining his plan, we started to work. During the next few days, we cut a hole in the back of the dummy and mounted two radio receivers inside him. We put a small speaker in his throat, and dressed him in overalls. When we got finished, he looked like any ordinary citizen of Mammoth Falls.

The night before Founders Day we were all ready. We met at the clubhouse late at night to carry the mannequin down to the Town Square.

Dinky Poore's little face screwed itself up into a doubting frown. "How we gonna get the dummy up on the monument? I'm not climbin' up there!"

"That's simple, stupid," said Freddy Muldoon, with a very superior air.

"Oh yeah?" Dinky puckered. "How would you do it, Mr. Great Brain?"

"That's easy," Freddy grunted. "I'd leave it to Henry, the Gentle Genius."

And that's just what he did.

Henry came up with a good plan, too — as he always does.

Hannah Kimball's monument stands in the center of a little park in front of the Town Hall. It's a slick marble column that goes 'way up in the air. Hannah Kimball herself stands at the top of it, holding her trusty blunderbuss at the ready. Somebody else could stand beside her if he could figure a way to get up there. Fortunately for us, there are telephone poles on either side of the park that are just a little taller than the monument is.

We showed up at the park late at night with about three hundred feet of good, stout piano rope. We looped a half-hitch around the dummy's neck and tied a length of clothesline to it for a guide rope. Two of us climbed up the telephone poles, which were right in line with the monument, and slipped the rope over the footspikes near the top of them. It was a simple matter to pull the rope taut from the ground; and the dummy was lofted into the air high enough to place him right on top of the monument by jockeying him into position with the guideline. Then we let the rope go at one end and pulled it free.

Early on the morning of Founders Day the

Flying Man was standing there with his hands on his hips. Since the monument is surrounded by trees, he wasn't noticed by anyone until the band marched up to the monument at ten o'clock. It was leading the parade that had started at the bridge over Lemon Creek.

Mortimer and Henry and I were sitting in the third-storey loft over Snodgrass' hardware store — the one that Homer's father owns. We had our transmitting gear with us, and we had a good view of the monument and the whole Square through the two little windows at the end of the loft. Homer was down in the Square, where he could keep an eye on developments and let us know what was happening. We could pick up most of the conversation over the microphones we had hidden around the monument.

Mayor Scragg and the Founders Day Committee were riding in an open car right behind the band. The Mayor was standing up on the back seat, waving his hat at the crowd and smiling in every direction. Suddenly a voice rang out above the cheers and the music.

"Look out, Mr. Mayor! I'm going to jump!"

The voice came out of the mannequin, but it was Mortimer Dalrymple's voice.

The Mayor's car came to a stop so suddenly

that he almost toppled into the front seat. The members of the Founders Day Committee grabbed hold of him to keep him from falling. They looked like the Marines trying to raise the flag on Iwo Jima. When the Mayor was upright again, he looked up and saw the mannequin at the top of the monument.

"How on earth did you get up there, young man?" he called out, shaking his umbrella furiously at the figure.

"I flew up here!" came the reply.

The Mayor looked at the members of the committee, and the members of the committee looked toward the chief of police, and the chief of police looked back at the Mayor. Mayor Scragg cleared his throat and flapped his cheeks in and out a few times, the way he always does when he doesn't know what to say. Then he leaned over and said very quietly to Chief Putney, "I think maybe we've got a nut on our hands."

"I agree," said Chief Putney. "Maybe if we ignore him he'll go away."

"Don't be silly," said the Mayor. "This kind doesn't go away. We've got to get him down from there before he ruins the whole Founders Day ceremony."

"What would you suggest, your Honor?"

"You're a chief of police," said the Mayor. "I'd suggest you start earning your salary." And the Mayor turned and smiled and waved at the crowds again.

"Did you call me a nut?" came the voice from the mannequin.

The Mayor looked up and flapped his cheeks in and out again.

"I'm not a nut. I'm a Mexican jumping bean," said the mannequin. "Wanna see me jump?"

By this time the open area around the monument had become crowded with people, all pushing against each other, trying to get a closer view of what was going on. The Mayor was still standing in the back seat of the open touring car, holding his arms up in the air and trying to get the crowd to be quiet. "Ladies and gentlemen!" he said, trying to sound as loud and important as he could.

"Ladies and gentlemen!" echoed the mannequin.

The Mayor looked up at the mannequin and said, "Shut up!"

"Shut up!" repeated the mannequin to the crowd. There was a great laugh.

"Fellow citizens!" said the Mayor.

"Fellow citizens!" said the mannequin.

"I implore you to pay no attention to the man on top of the monument," said the Mayor. "Your able chief of police, Harold Putney, and the fire department, I am sure, will manage to get him down safely."

"If they come near me I'll jump!" said the mannequin.

The Mayor flapped his cheeks in and out again.

"Pay no attention to that unfortunate man up there," he said. "He needs all the help and understanding we can give him."

"I don't need help, but you do!" said the mannequin.

By this time Henry and I were laughing so hard Mortimer could hardly keep his face straight. He had to shut off the transmitter until we calmed down. The crowd was milling around Mayor Scragg's car, making suggestions about how to get the nut down off the monument. A bunch of kids were standing on the bleachers at the edge of the crowd yelling for him to jump.

"When'll we let him go?" I asked.

"Pretty quick now. Then we'll turn the show back to his Honor," said Henry.

He switched on the ham outfit. "We'd better see if we can reach Jeff and the others."

Jeff and Dinky and Freddy Muldoon were supposed to be somewhere out west of Strawberry Lake. When Henry reached them, they were sitting on a hilltop where they could see the Town Hall and the Square through binoculars. Henry checked the wind direction from the weather vane on top of Town Hall and suggested to Jeff that they move to another hill a little farther south. This was important to our plan.

We looked out on the Square again, and the crowd was still milling about, pointing up at the dummy and hollering to him. He just stood there with his hands on his hips, the way we had placed him, leaning slightly against the barrel of Hannah Kimball's blunderbuss.

Then we heard the wail of a siren and the clang of a bell as the Mammoth Falls fire department's hook and ladder nosed its way through the crowd. Mayor Scragg stepped down out of the automobile and directed operations with his hat as he waved the hook and ladder into position.

They maneuvered the huge truck close to the monument and extended the ladder up its side. Mayor Scragg stood up in the cab of the fire engine and shouted to the mannequin.

"And now, sir, will you please come down from there?"

"Will you promise not to bite me?"

The crowd roared again. Mayor Scragg flushed red and harrumphed.

"See here, young man. I'm not in a habit of biting people. Just come down the ladder and no one will hurt you."

"I don't climb ladders. I'm an eagle!" said the mannequin.

Mayor Scragg harrumphed again and tried to quiet the crowd.

"Do you want to see me fly?" cried the mannequin. At this point Mortimer let out with a hyena yell and shouted "Geronimo!" at the top of his lungs.

"No! No!" screamed the Mayor. "Wait a minute!"

The Mayor turned and looked at the Founders Day Committee, and the committee turned and looked at Chief Putney, and Chief Putney turned and looked at Constable Billy Dahr. Constable Dahr had a mustache that drooped over the corners of his mouth. He always wore a coat that hung down to his knees and carried a billy club clasped behind him that he'd waggle back and forth like a tail. When he found everybody looking at him, he waggled the billy club faster than ever and looked behind him as if he was trying to see who the chief was looking at.

"Constable Dahr will go up and get the man," said Chief Putney.

"Just the man to do it, Mr. Putney," agreed the Mayor. And the committee nodded approval.

Billy Dahr pretended he couldn't hear what was being said to him. But finally he started to scale the ladder with great care and caution. He ascended three steps and paused there, brandishing his club.

"Now, you come down here, young man!" he said.

"If you come up here I'll pull your mustache with both hands," the mannequin shouted.

The crowd roared with laughter. Mayor Scragg was furious. He started poking Constable Dahr in the seat of the pants with his umbrella.

"Get on up there, Constable! Get on up there!"

"It's no use, Mr. Mayor," Billy Dahr complained. "I get dizzy from vertigo in high places."

"Oh, for heaven's sakes," said the Mayor.

By this time the fire chief had arrived on the scene and was conferring with Chief Putney. Chief Putney went over and said something to the Mayor that we couldn't hear, and the Mayor nodded. The next thing we knew, four groups of firemen were breaking out jumping nets. They stretched them out on all sides of the monument, with volunteers from the crowd helping to hold them. Two firemen started up the ladder, a third one following them with a straitjacket. Chief Putney and Constable Dahr were moving people back, clear of the monument.

"Hurry up, Mortimer," said Henry, "or we'll be in the soup."

Mortimer flicked on his mike. "Get back down that ladder!" he hollered. "If you come near me I'll jump!"

The firemen stopped. Mayor Scragg fumed.

"Get on up there, men!" said the fire chief. "If he jumps, we'll catch him in one of the nets."

"Who's going to catch *them*?" asked the mannequin.

The firemen stopped again. Finally, under the urging of their chief, they proceeded cautiously toward the top of the ladder, gently coaxing the mannequin to give himself up quietly.

When the lead fireman was three or four rungs from the top, Mortimer cut loose with a final "Geronimo!" and Henry flipped a switch on the transmitter that was tuned to the second receiver hidden inside the dummy. There was a sharp explosion like the pop of a medium-sized Fourth of July firecracker, and a package shot out from the back of the dummy. It fell about halfway down the side of the monument, and dangled there for a moment at the end of a bundle of stout cords. Then, slowly, it expanded into the shape of a balloon and, growing ever larger, began to rise slowly upward.

The stunned firemen stood stock-still on the ladder. A hush fell over the crowd. Then an incredulous roar burst from it as the balloon swelled to huge proportions and soared upward on a gust of wind. It lifted the dummy clear of the monument, while cries of "I'm an eagle! I'm an eagle!" issued from its throat. It gained altitude rapidly and went careening off across the Town Square, heading toward the lake.

Henry and Mortimer and I were jumping up and down at the windows of the loft, slapping each other on the back and laughing till our sides ached. The stunt had worked perfectly, and Henry's wizardry had paid off for us again. The surplus weather balloon we had strapped to the dummy's back had been inflated by a capsule of compressed helium. Henry had rigged the firing mechanism from a CO_2 pistol so that it punctured the capsule with a small firing pin when the radio signal from our transmitter fired the charge that propelled the balloon out of its package.

Out on the Square, confusion reigned. The crowd had started to break up at the fringes as people ran pell-mell down side streets, trying to keep the intrepid balloonist in sight.

"Get on the air, Mortimer," Henry commanded. "We've got to keep in touch with Jeff if we don't want to lose half our radio gear."

Mortimer flipped on our outfit to get through to Jeff, and Henry started monitoring the police and emergency bands to see what information he could pick up. With binoculars and a compass I kept an eye on our flying mannequin. He was flying pretty high now, and was being blown out across Strawberry Lake just about the way we had figured.

Homer Snodgrass reported up from the Square that Mayor Scragg was in a real tizzy. He had ordered the civil defense units into full alert, and had told Chief Putney to notify the Air Force at Westport Field what had happened.

Henry picked up Chief Putney's transmission to Westport Field. He requested two helicopters to track the balloonist until he came down, so they could see that he got into the proper institution. The operator at Westport Field wouldn't believe him at first, but promised to relay the information to Colonel March, the base commander, anyway. Two minutes later we monitored a transmission from Westport Field on the emergency band. Colonel March was notifying all the stations in his net.

"Unidentified flying man sighted proceeding west out of Mammoth Falls. Sightings reported by police department, Mammoth Falls, and one airline pilot. Exact heading and altitude unknown. Destination unknown. No flight plan filed at this facility nor at local airport. Request reports of further sightings. Please stand by. Over and out."

We practically went through the roof of Mr. Snodgrass' loft when we heard this. Henry was in a sweat.

"We've got to work fast," he said. "I hope Colonel March doesn't find out we're behind this. He'll raise holy Ned with us."

One minute later Henry was sweating even more. Westport Field announced to all the stations in its net that it was scrambling two search craft and a helicopter team to see if it could confirm sightings of the unidentified flying man.

"Can you get a reading on the dummy?" Henry cried.

The dummy was silhouetted against a good cloud background right at that point. I took a sighting with my compass.

"Looks like two hundred and sixty-five degrees," I told Henry. "As far as I can tell, that's the direction he's drifting, and he's just about reached the lake."

"Good," said Henry. "We shall still have time."

He drew a line quickly on the map he had with him, and then grabbed for the hand set of the citizens' band transceiver.

"Grand Vizier to High Mogul!"

"Come in, Grand Vizier. This is High Mogul."

"Jeff! You'll have to get back to the hill where you were before. I figure you've got about six minutes. The dummy's coming in on a heading of two hundred and sixty-five degrees. That's eighty-five degrees from where you'll be. Let me know as soon as you sight him. And let me know as soon as he's overhead, so I can push the button."

"You're making it rough on us, Henry. Over and out."

Out on the Square we could hear the wail of sirens. Every ambulance in town seemed to be moving out on the road toward Strawberry Lake. Other cars were following, and still more were taking the road north of the lake in case the dummy drifted that way. Mayor Scragg was still standing near the monument, directing operations and waving his umbrella at all and sundry. The Founders Day ceremonies were completely forgotten.

"You've got to hand it to Mayor Scragg," said Mortimer. "He's got this town moving."

"That's going to make it rough on us," said Henry. "I didn't think he'd get things organized so fast."

Jeff's voice came over the receiver. "High Mogul to Grand Vizier! Come in! Come in!"

"This is Grand Vizier. Go ahead!"

"We're back on the other hill."

"Can you see the dummy?"

"Yes! He's getting close to this side of the lake. He's coming right toward us, but we're going to have to move down the hill to our right a bit. Don't cut it loose till I give you the signal."

"O.K.! We're standing by."

"This is going to be a near thing," Henry said. "Those search planes from Westport Field should be getting out over the lake soon. If the helicopters get in close enough to see what we're doing, it may spoil our whole plan."

"Let's not get Colonel March mad at us," said Mortimer. "He's done us a lot of favors."

"That's just what I'm worried about!" said Henry.

The Town Square was completely deserted now. Even Mayor Scragg had left to join the search parties that were hoping to track the balloonist to a landing somewhere in the wooded hills west of Strawberry Lake. I kept my binoculars frozen on the figure of the dummy and fed Henry information on his course and position.

Two search planes were already circling high above the dummy. Off to the north I could see the two helicopters form Westport Field churning their way south. In three or four minutes they would be at the other side of the lake.

"Better hurry," I said to Henry. "The choppers are closing in fast."

Just then Jeff's voice came over the receiver.

"He's just a little way from us now, Henry. You can drop him any time."

"O.K.," said Henry. "But keep under cover of the trees and work fast. There are two planes overhead right now, and there'll be two choppers on top of you in no time!"

Henry flipped a switch on our big transmitter and then ran to join me at the window. We saw the balloon jerk violently and begin to collapse. The charge Henry had wired to a second receiver

126

inside it had blown a small hole in its side. The dummy sank rapidly toward the earth as the balloon folded in on itself. We lost sight of it in the trees.

What happened from then on we knew only through Jeff's radio reports. The dummy came swinging down faster than we had expected it would. Jeff and Freddy and Dinky watched it careening dizzily toward the side of the hill they were on, and hoped it would land in a soft place so the radio parts inside it wouldn't be smashed to bits. They scrambled down the hill in time to see it crash through a bushy maple. The balloon snagged itself in the branches, and the dummy jerked up short on the end of its shrouds, dangling twenty feet from the ground.

"Get up there and cut the balloon loose. We've got to get it out of sight!" Jeff shouted, as he boosted Dinky up the tree.

Little Dinky skinned up the maple like a wildcat. He was quick as a fox and skinny enough to worm his way through the tightest places. In a few seconds he had cut the balloon free with his Scout knife and Freddy and Jeff caught the dummy in their arms. Dinky was down out of the tree like a monkey, and the three of them took off through the woods for the cave where they had hidden their bicycles.

The cave was an unfinished shaft that had been abandoned when they stopped working the old zinc mine in that area. It's overgrown with bushes now, but a spur track leads from it to an old crusher; and from there a rusty, abandoned rail line runs due north to where it joins up with the main line just outside of Hyattsville.

When the dummy emerged from the cave, he was wearing the uniform of an Explorer Scout, just like the rest of the boys. He was lashed to the baggage rack of Jeff's bicycle, with his arms tied tight around Jeff's waist. With knapsacks and fishing rods to complete the ensemble, the whole group looked as though they were just returning from an overnight camping trip. They pedaled down the abandoned rail line, Jeff in the lead.

As they turned onto Turkey Hill Road, which leads back to town along the north shore of the lake, they began to pass some of the convoy vehicles that had brought search parties out to the scene. The antiquated touring car that had carried Mayor Scragg in the parade came charging around a bend.

"Get those bikes off the road, boys!" the Mayor shouted. "This is an emergency."

"Yes, sir," said Dinky. "We're getting back to town as fast as fast as we can." And he kept right on pedaling.

"Have you seen a man in blue overalls anywhere around here?" the Mayor shouted at Freddy Muldoon.

Freddy shouted back over his shoulder, "We haven't seen a living soul." And that was no lie.

A quarter of a mile farther down the road a blue Air Force sedan braked to a lurching stop. The driver put it in reverse and backed up fast. Colonel March's head popped out of the rear window.

"Hello, boys!" The Colonel was smiling.

Jeff kinda waved at him, with a grin that looked as if he was sick to his stomach, and kept right on pedaling. Dinky Poore, whose legs aren't long enough for him to sit on his seat, almost fell off his bike trying to give the Colonel a big salute as he chugged on past. But the Colonel reached out and stopped Freddy Muldoon.

"Who's the big boy riding with Jeff?" he asked.

"Oh, him? . . . Oh, he's a friend of ours," said Freddy. "I think he's staying with Henry Mulligan."

"That's nice," said the Colonel. "Where's he from?"

"Henry lives right here in Mammoth Falls."

"I know that," said the Colonel. "I mean the new boy."

"Oh, him? . . . I don't know," said Freddy, "I think he's from Canada. . . . Maybe England. I don't think you'd wanna meet him, Colonel."

"Oh, I see. He seems like a pretty big fellow. I just wondered why he didn't have a bike of his own, that's all."

"He's sick!" said Freddy. "Well . . . I mean . . . well, Colonel, you gotta realize, in some foreign countries people don't have very much money."

"Oh yes! I understand that's the case," said the Colonel. "Well, he seemed like a very nice young man. I just thought I'd like to meet him sometime."

"Oh, he is a very nice fellow," said Freddy. "He's not the least bit nosy, either!"

"I see what you mean," said the Colonel. "Well, good-bye, Freddy. Nice talking to you."

"Good-bye, Colonel!"

And Freddy took off like a jet to catch up with Dinky and Jeff.

Back in the loft over Mr. Snodgrass' hardware store, the rest of us had not been idle. The Town Square was completely deserted, except for Constable Billy Dahr, who had fallen asleep in the sun on the Town Hall steps. As soon as the coast was clear, Homer Snodgrass had shinnied up one of the telephone poles again and looped a length of piano wire over the topmost footspike. The other end of the loop ran through a pulley we'd nailed fast to the wall of the loft.

When Jeff and Dinky and Freddy got back with the Flying Man, we pulled all our radio gear out of him and put him back into his blue overalls. Then we hooked him onto the piano wire with a guide line attached. We pushed him out through the window and gave him a breeches buoy ride back out to the monument. It was easy to lower him by his own weight back into the cradle formed by Hannah Kimball's arms. Then we just cut the piano wire so it dangled free, and pulled the loose end in through the window.

We had barely gotten the piano wire back inside, and closed the loft window, when we saw Billy Dahr yawn and stretch himself on the Town Hall steps. All of a sudden he catapulted his creaky frame into the middle of the street and stood there gaping at the monument, his billy club in one hand and his false teeth in the other. He rubbed his eyes with the back of his hands and looked again. He looked all around the Town Square to make sure no one was there.

Then he took off and high-tailed it down the street to the firehouse at the corner.

A half hour later the Square was full of people again. Mayor Scragg's deep-breathing touring car pulled up in front of the monument, and shortly afterward the hook-and-ladder rig arrived. The firemen lost no time in cranking the ladder up the side of the marble shaft again, and two of them dashed up it pell-mell with the straitjacket. This time there was not a word from the man on the monument. He seemed to have lost his voice.

The lead fireman lunged up the last few rungs of the ladder and pinned the dummy against the statue of Hannah Kimball with both hands. Then he stepped back and stared at it. Suddenly he stepped forward and grabbed the dummy by the neck. There was a horrified scream from the crowd as he flung it from the top of the monument. It landed with a dull thud in one of the lifesaving nets.

Curious spectators crowded around the net to get a closer look at the man who had been thrown into it.

Mayor Scragg looked at it and said, "Hurrumph!"

He poked at it gingerly with the tip of his umbrella. Then he snorted, and stalked off into the

Town Hall. The crowd of spectators gradually thinned out; and as twilight fell on the Square, Mike Corcoran could be seen walking toward his pool hall on Blake Street with the Unidentified Flying Man tucked under his arm.

Next day the ceremonies went off pretty well. Mayor Scragg got a bad crick in his neck from looking up at the top of the monument all the time, to see if the Flying Man was there again; but otherwise things went according to schedule.

Colonel March was there, and he took advantage of the Mayor's invitation to give a short speech on preparedness. He told everybody that the day was past when we could rely on stunts like Hannah Kimball's to defend ourselves. And he said that an important part of being prepared was to be ready for the unexpected. These days we have to look for a lot of unexpected things to happen; and when they do, we have to learn to accept them and not get panicky. He thought that yesterday's incident of the Unidentified Flying Man might serve as a good object lesson for everybody to think about.

After the ceremonies were over, and the politicians had shaken hands all around, Colonel March came over to where we were sitting in the bleachers. He looked right at Henry Mulligan.

"What happened to your friend from Canada?"

he asked. "I thought maybe I'd get a chance to meet him."

"What friend?" said Henry.

"The one I saw riding on the bicycle with Jeff yesterday," said the Colonel.

"Oh, *that* one!" Henry looked around at all the rest of us. "Well, to tell you the truth, Colonel — "

"He died last night!" said Freddy Muldoon.

"I'm glad to hear that," said the Colonel. "I mean, that's too bad! I'm sorry."

"Yes! It was very sad," said Freddy.

"He didn't look too healthy when I saw him," said the Colonel.

"He was real sick," said Freddy Muldoon.

"Well, please extend my condolences to his family," the Colonel said, with a wink.

"We will!"

And that was the last that Colonel March ever said on the subject.

But the mystery of the Unidentified Flying Man still lives in Mammoth Falls. People still argue about it. Half of them believe there was a real man on the monument in the first place and somebody just dressed a dummy up to look like him afterward. Others think there were two dummies, and some ventriloquist in the crowd was just making the first one talk. But nobody can explain what happened to the first dummy, or the balloon, which has never been found.

Those who argue about it usually end up at Mike Corcoran's pool hall, where the Unidentified Flying Man still stands today in the front window. Mike had a sign painted that stands at the dummy's feet. It says:

DON'T BE A SUCKER FOR A SCARE-CROW!

The Great Gas Bag Race

Zeke Boniface wears winter underwear all year
long. The reason we know is that in summer
he doesn't wear any shirt. You can always tell how
long he's had the underwear on by the different
color that shows at the beltline when he bends
over to pick something up. The top two buttons
are always unbuttoned and the hairs of his chest
stick out there.

But Zeke runs the most wonderful junk yard
in the world. You can find anything if you look
long enough. Whenever you ask him for something he'll roll the stub of his cigar from one side
of his mouth to the other and scratch his mustache with one finger. Then he'll push his bat-
tered old black derby up off his forehead and

scratch his head, as if he never heard of the thing you're asking for. But sooner or later, he'll recollect seeing something like what you want, and he'll lead the way to one of the mountains of cluttered junk that crowd his yard.

Zeke never touches any of the junk himself. He just shows you where it is, and then stands there talking about where he picked up a particular piece while you rummage through the pile to pull out what you want.

That was how we found the World War II inflatable life raft for the gondola of the balloon Henry Mulligan designed for the Great Gas Bag Race.

Every year Mammoth Falls is host for the County Fair, and ever since anyone can remember there's been some kind of a race on opening day. It used to be a horse and buggy race, and then for a long time they ran it with farm tractors. But lately it's been a balloon race, and people come from all over the state to see it. If the wind is blowing in the usual direction, it starts in White Fork, about fifty miles away, and ends up at the fair grounds.

Most of the balloons don't make it, because they run out of ballast or their gas leaks out long before they get to Mammoth Falls. Sometimes the sheriff's office and the state police spend the whole day trying to find the people who come down in the woods or in the hills between here and White Fork. Once in a while somebody gets real lost and spends the whole night trying to find his way back to town.

Henry figured the Mad Scientists' Club ought to be a cinch to win the race, because he had an idea for a balloon that didn't need any ballast and could stay up practically forever.

"What kinda balloon are we gonna make?" asked Freddy Muldoon between sniffles. Freddy had a bad cold.

"Never you mind," said Henry. "You'll find out after it's all built. Meanwhile I don't want it blabbermouthed all over town. Harmon is entering a balloon in the race too, and we don't want him stealing our ideas."

"Who else is going to ride in it?" asked Dinky Poore. Dinky, being our smallest member, knew he was a cinch to be a passenger.

Jeff Crocker rapped his gavel on the table. "As president, I appoint Henry Mulligan to figure that out," he said, "and whatever he decides is what we'll do!"

"That's all got to be figured out real scientific,"

said Freddy Muldoon, looking at Dinky Poore as though he hadn't grown up yet.

The next three weeks we were pretty busy. We knew we faced some stiff competition, because there were a lot of old-time balloonists entered in the race. Mike Corcoran, who runs the Idle Hour Pool Palace down on Baker Street, was sponsoring Harmon Muldoon's entry. We knew that Mike wanted to win the race for the sake of the publicity, and he was willing to put up a lot of money to make sure Harmon had the best balloon in the field of entries. We figured it was a case of Henry Mulligan's brains against all the money Harmon had behind him.

But where science is concerned, brains can make up for a lot of money, and we all had faith in Henry.

We built our balloon up in the loft over Mr. Snodgrass' hardware store. We didn't want to build it in Jeff Crocker's barn because some member of Harmon's gang is always hanging around trying to spy on what we're doing. The loft over Snodgrass' Hardware is on the third floor, and it's pretty hard to spy on anything going on there.

One thing about balloons you've got to be careful about — they're great Yo-yos. They can swing you up into the sky in a hurry, and then drop you back down again just as fast. Henry says it has something to do with the equilibrium between a body and the medium it's floating in. As long as your balloon weighs just a little less than the air it displaces, you're fine. It'll float along just a little way above the earth and not give you any trouble. But if the temperature rises, or an updraft catches you, you can zoom right up to twenty thousand feet and find yourself gasping for breath. When the updraft leaves you, or the temperature cools off, you find you've got the proverbial "lead balloon" on your hands, and you start losing altitude like crazy. The balloon doesn't just float back down to where it belongs. Gravity pulls it down so fast that it'll crash right into the ground if you don't have some kind of ballast to throw overboard, or some other means of increasing your lift.

Most balloonists figure to compensate for this by letting some of the gas out of the bag when they're rising too fast, or dumping sandbags overboard when they're dropping too fast. The big problem, of course, is that they eventually run out of gas, or sand, and they can't control the altitude of the balloon. Then they have to ditch it and give up. In a fifty-mile race, it's a good bet that better than ninety per cent of the balloons won't finish.

Henry figured he had this problem licked, and this was our big secret.

Henry's mother complains that he'd rather think than eat. Sometimes he'll start thinking right in the middle of supper. He'll push his plate aside and he won't take another bite until he's figured out a problem that's on his mind. When she nags him about not touching his food, he slips it under the table to the family dog while her back is turned. The Mulligans have the fattest dog in the neighborhood.

Some people think Henry's a nut. But to him food isn't that important. You gotta eat enough to keep strong, he always says, but don't let it go to your head. It all depends on whether you want to be a scientist when you grow up or the fat man of the circus.

Freddy Muldoon is different. He's always thinking too, but usually it's about food. When he asked Henry if he could be one of the flight crew on the balloon, Henry told him we didn't need that much ballast.

Henry's idea was really quite simple. Most great ideas are. He figured you could keep a balloon under control if you could just vary the size of it by pumping gas in and out of the bag. Then you wouldn't need any ballast. With a couple of pressure tanks in the gondola and a good compressor, you could pump gas back into the tanks when you wanted to go down, and let it expand into the balloon again when you wanted to go up.

We made the envelope for our balloon out of silk from surplus parachutes and inflated it in Jeff Crocker's barn in order to paint it. If you've never painted a balloon, don't try it. It's a lot worse than painting a house. There isn't any way to climb up on it; and even if you could, there isn't any way to keep yourself from falling off. Dinky Poore did most of the painting, slung in a big trash can hanging from a rope hung over the rafters in Jeff's barn.

Later we trucked the thing out to a clearing in the hills back of Strawberry Lake for some captive flight tests. Henry's calculations proved to be just about right. The balloon had over six hundred pounds of lift, which was enough to carry three of us in the gondola, along with the two pressure tanks for the helium supply, the gasoline-driven compressor, and a little miscellaneous gear. We floated it about a hundred feet in the air, tied down with long ropes, so Henry could experiment with the compressor and get an idea how rapidly the balloon would gain or lose altitude. He also had us tie it down with just one rope attached to a spring scale, so we could measure the amount of lift it had under full load.

When we got all through with the captive trials, Henry was satisfied. "I've studied the terrain between White Fork and the fair grounds," he said, "and I figure we've got to stay at about twelve hundred feet to clear the highest hills. But we've got enough lift to float at two thousand, if everything works perfectly and the weather conditions are ideal."

"Two thousand feet is nothin'," said Freddy Muldoon.

"It is if you have to step out at the end of the line," said Mortimer Dalrymple.

"Why two thousand feet, Henry?" I asked.

"At this time of year, on clear days, there's a fast-moving layer of air at that altitude. It might move us along at twenty-five or thirty miles an hour, right toward the fair grounds. I checked all this with the meteorologist at Westport Field."

"Better not let Harmon Muldoon know that," said Dinky.

"Shucks, I'll bet we're not the only ones that know it," said Homer Snodgrass. "There's a lot of old-time balloonists in this race. They know all about the weather and the winds around here."

"Sure, they do," Henry observed, "but the big question is whether they can get up to two thousand feet and stay there. I figure *we* can if there are just three of us in the gondola, and one of them has to be you, Dinky."

"Aw, nuts!" said Freddy Muldoon.

We all knew that Henry had to be the second one, so the rest of us drew lots to see who would be lucky number three, and I got the long straw.

"Nuts!" said Freddy Muldoon.

The night before the big race, Zeke Boniface hauled us and all our gear over to White Fork in Richard the Deep Breather. We camped out on the grounds of the race track, where the balloons would start from, so we could be up early in the morning. There's a lot of work to be done before you can get a balloon off the ground. They just don't go up by themselves.

Naturally, we didn't sleep too much. There were a lot of other groups there making preparations for the launching in the morning, and Homer Snodgrass kept circulating among them, picking up gossip and information. Homer was particularly interested, because Daphne Muldoon, still his girl friend, would be selected

Queen of the County Fair if our balloon won the race.

There were about twenty balloons entered in the race, and they were painted all the colors of the rainbow and then some. Some of them were decorated to look like Christmas-tree ornaments, and others like spinning tops. There was one that looked like a big fish and another one shaped like a big green caterpillar. Harmon Muldoon called his the "Green Onion," and it looked like one.

"I hope it springs a leek," quipped Dinky Poore, when he first saw it.

Our own balloon had a face painted on it that looked a little bit like Mayor Scragg. We called it "The Head." The nose on the face marked the location of the rip panel. You have to have a rip panel in case you get caught in a high wind near the ground and you want to let all the gas out of your balloon at once. Otherwise you might get dragged for miles, and smash up against trees and rocks.

The race was slated to start at eight o'clock sharp, and as early as 4 A.M. a lot of ground crews were already inflating their balloons and tying them down to stakes driven into the ground. Henry said we'd wait until well after sunrise to inflate The Head; because there was usually a strong wind about the time the sun came up, and with the temperature rising about twenty degrees, a lot of the crews were going to have a tough time holding their balloons on the ground. He proved right, too.

Harmon Muldoon's gang came over to look at our balloon and kid us as much as they could. We had it spread out on the ground, ready to inflate and weighted down with rocks and boards.

"You guys keep quiet!" said Jeff Crocker, when he saw them coming. "Let Henry and me do the talking. We don't want to get a fight started."

"Well, if that isn't the most!" said Stony Martin, who is known as a loudmouth even in Harmon Muldoon's gang.

"The most what?" chorused the rest of the gang.

"The most flattest balloon I ever saw!" said Stony, kicking one edge of the envelope. This was greeted with a loud guffaw.

"When you stop laughing, supposing you tell me what we can do for you," said Jeff, lounging back against his sleeping bag. "Did you come over for some advice?"

Harmon Muldoon bristled. He stood before Jeff with his fists dug into his hips. "We just came

146

over to see if you were carrying any BB guns or sling shots," he said. "They're outlawed, you know."

"Do tell!" sighed Mortimer Dalrymple, breathing on his fingernails and polishing them on his shirt front.

"Oh, my gracious!" said Freddy Muldoon, with a loud sniffle. "That reminds me. I forgot to bring my bow and arrows!"

"I thought I told you guys to cool it," said Jeff, getting to his feet. He looked Harmon Muldoon straight in the eye. "If we win this race, Harmon, we'll win it fair and square. That's the only way we want it."

"We're not worried about you winning it," snorted Stony Martin. "We just want you to keep out of our way — that is, if you manage to get this sad sack off the ground."

"If we get in your way, write us a letter about it," said Mortimer, stifling a yawn.

"Stow it, Mortimer!" Jeff warned.

"What's your crew gonna ride in?" asked Harmon. "I don't see any gondola around here."

"This is our gondola," said Henry, tapping the bundle he was leaning against.

"What is it?"

"It's an inflatable life raft," said Henry. "Or

didn't you know that you have to fly right across Strawberry Lake to get to the fair grounds?"

"We know it," shouted Stony with great glee, "but we're not planning on making any stops!"

After the laughter had died down, Henry smiled quietly. "Judging from your conversation, I assume you're using hot air for gas," he said coolly.

"Maybe you can talk your way across the lake!" chirped Dinky Poore.

"That'll be enough of that!" said Jeff, standing up to his full height and looking down on Harmon Muldoon. "I think our guests are leaving. Nice of you to drop by, fellows!"

As the group shuffled off, Stony Martin aimed a rabbit punch at the back of Dinky Poore's neck. But somehow his feet went out from under him and he hit the ground with a thud.

"Excuse me!" said Mortimer Dalrymple, pulling his legs out of the way and handing Stony his hat. "For a minute I thought you'd lost your head!"

As soon as the sun came up, a pretty strong wind blew in from the east, just as Henry said it would. A lot of the crews had trouble keeping their balloons tied down. Two of them broke their moorings completely. They went careening across the race track and got fouled up in the woods on the other side of the railroad tracks.

"Scratch two balloons," said Henry. "They'll never get those repaired in time to get in the race."

Later we wandered over to see how Harmon Muldoon's gang was doing with the Green Onion. Sure enough, they were in trouble. They had to let some of the gas out of their bag to keep it from lifting off, and it had pulled out several of the mooring stakes. When we got there, the whole gang was flailing around trying to keep the rig from blowing away. Everybody had hold of a rope, trying to snub the lines shorter and tie the balloon closer to the ground. The huge bag was pitching and tossing in the wind like a cork on a stormy sea.

"You'll never do it that way," shouted Henry. "Work on one rope at a time!"

Just then a strong gust of wind shot the balloon skyward. Two of the crew lost their footing and were dragged across the ground until they let go of the ropes. Another mooring line snapped loose from the balloon. Stony Martin, with a rope coiled tightly around his left arm, was jerked off his feet and whipped sideways in a wide, sweeping curve. Only one line remained tied to a stake, and the force of the balloon's oscillations was working the stake loose from the ground. Stony was dangling six feet in the air, his legs kicking wildly, trying to find something solid to hold on to.

"That bag sure went up with a jerk!" snorted Dinky Poore.

Jeff Crocker dashed forward and aimed a flying tackle at Stony's legs. He caught him around the knees and brought him crashing to the ground. Before they could get to their feet another gust of wind shot the balloon upward again.

"Go get Zeke and the truck!" cried Mortimer, giving Dinky Poore a shove. Then he and Henry ran to the lone mooring stake and threw their weight on it. Homer Snodgrass and I dove for another line and dug our heels into the ground as best we could.

The rest of Harmon's gang staggered to their feet in bewilderment and tried to help out. They all managed to get hold of a piece of rope, but a balloon in a high wind is like a bucking bronco. We were just barely holding our own when Dinky got back with Zeke Boniface and Richard the Deep Breather in a whirling cloud of dust. Zeke brought the ancient truck to a skidding stop directly under the balloon, stepped up on the seat, and snaked one mooring line out of the air with a hamlike fist. With his leg hooked through the steering wheel, he gave a mighty tug on the rope and dragged the balloon and all the rest of us in his direction. Then he cinched the rope around the steering column and jumped to the back of the truck, where he made another line fast to the tailgate. The balloon still whipped angrily back and forth, but it was held fast to the ground by the sheer weight of Richard the Deep Breather.

"Gee! Thanks!" said Harmon Muldoon, after we had the balloon staked to the ground again and the wind had died down a bit.

"Don't mention it!" said Jeff Crocker. "Funny thing about a balloon. One minute you can't hold it down, and the next thing you know, you can't get it off the ground."

"We won't have any trouble getting off the ground!" shouted Stony Martin as we moved away.

"Rots of ruck!" said Freddy Muldoon, shouting back.

It was well after sunrise when we started inflating The Head. The wind had dropped to a gentle breeze and the weather looked good. We had just about an hour till lift-off time. As usual, Henry made us go through a checkout procedure, by the numbers, for every phase of the operation. It sounded just like the countdown for a missile launching.

"It's the only way to make sure you aren't forgetting something," Henry explained. "When you have a lot of things to remember, it's easy to forget one of them. But if you assign every step a number, then it's a cinch. It's pretty hard to forget that 4 comes between 3 and 5."

The hot-air balloons were inflating too, and by the time the sun was fully up, the White Fork race track looked like a fantastic fairyland of bright-colored silk. Balloons and tents were everywhere, and people were streaming onto the grounds from every direction to see the start of the race. Dinky Poore was sitting on his knapsack with his eyes popped wide open and his chin in his hands.

"Gosh!" he said. "Charlemagne's army must have looked just like this when it started getting ready for battle."

"Charlie who?" grunted Freddy Muldoon.

"Shut up, you goofball!" said Dinky, and went right on staring at the balloons and the crowds.

Suddenly the loudspeakers started to crackle and a race official began giving instructions to the balloon crews. There was a noticeable change in the movement of the crowd of spectators as they sensed the race was about to begin. They began filing out of the center oval toward the stands and the railing that circled the track. It seemed as though everyone had a camera or a pair of binoculars, or both. Telescopes and cameras were being set up on tripods all over the place. Some people had even gotten up onto the roof of the stands and were setting up movie cameras, until the White Fork police chased them off.

All of a sudden it was for real. After all the weeks of preparation and planning and dreaming, The Head was just a few minutes away from her first flight. I could feel a big hollow place in the pit of my stomach, and I noticed that Henry kept taking his glasses off and wiping them for no reason at all.

The mayor of White Fork got up in the officials' stand and introduced Mayor Scragg of Mammoth Falls. Then the two of them introduced the girls who were candidates for Queen of the County Fair. Each girl had to give a speech and throw a rose to the captain of the balloon crew that sponsored her. If the rose hit the ground it was considered bad luck. Stony Martin's girl friend, Melissa Plunkett, gave a good speech, but her aim was bad and Harmon Muldoon fell flat on his face diving for the rose. He got it, though, and he and his crew dashed off and climbed into the gondola of the Green Onion.

"You gotta hand it to Stony," sighed Mortimer Dalrymple. "That Melissa is a real knockout!"

"Her teeth stick out too much," said Dinky Poore.

When Daphne Muldoon was introduced, we whistled and cheered and stamped our feet. She blew Homer a kiss before she tossed the rose, and he was still standing there blushing and digging his toe in the ground when we all took off for our balloon.

Dinky and Henry and I scrambled into the gondola, and the rest of the crew started checking the mooring lines. According to the rules, we had to keep four lines tied down until the starting gun sounded. Henry was fidgeting nervously with the quick-release buckles and checking the pressure gauges on the helium tanks. Jeff Crocker, with his arm raised in the air, was keeping one eye glued on the officials' stand.

We saw a checkered flag go up at the end of the line of balloons. A puff of smoke rose from the officials' stand, followed by the thin crack of a pistol shot. It didn't sound very loud, and we couldn't believe the race had started, until a roar went up from the stands and we saw one balloon rise up from the middle of the line.

"Cut her loose!" Jeff shouted, and jumped back from the gondola.

We flipped the levers on the release buckles and The Head shot upward for a few feet, then keeled over sideways and started spinning slowly counterclockwise. One rope still held her fast, and Dinky Poore was trying frantically to spring the buckle loose. I reached over and pulled with all my might on the release lever, but the buckle had been bent by the force of the balloon's pull, and it wouldn't budge. Out of the corner of my eye I saw Zeke Boniface step forward, and the blade of his hunting knife flashed in the sun. With one swipe he severed the rope, and The Head shot skyward for a moment, then jerked sideways and started to climb at a steep angle as the wind caught it and pushed it toward Mammoth Falls. We were on our way.

Henry was crouched on the floor of the gondola, glancing at his watch, then at the altimeter, then at the pressure gauges for the helium tanks and the balloon envelope. Dinky and I were leaning over the railing, waving wildly at the shrinking figures of the ground crew.

Suddenly the gondola lurched and swung crazily under our feet. A big orange balloon shot up from underneath us and bumped us again before it bounced free and went soaring straight up.

"Whew! That was close!" said Henry. "They're rising too fast. They'll have to let some gas out in a hurry if they want to keep her under control."

There hadn't been time to see what had happened to the Green Onion. The air was full of balloons, some rising lazily, some soaring rapidly, and some bouncing along the ground while their crews threw everything overboard, trying to get them aloft.

Our gondola pitched wildly again, as a heavy gust of wind hit us and drove us before it. Two of the balloons that were having trouble getting off the ground got caught in it and went careening across the fields and crashed into the woods the other side of the railroad track. One of them collapsed completely, and all we could see of it were the torn shreds of its envelope hanging from the limbs of the trees as we sailed overhead.

Dinky and I kept rubbernecking around, trying to catch sight of the Green Onion, but there was too much going on at once. The big orange balloon had climbed far above us and was now moving toward Mammoth Falls at a rapid rate. It was already about a mile ahead of us. Henry pointed upward.

"They've caught that layer of fast-moving air that we want to get into," he said. "But they're still climbing too fast. They'll climb right up out of it in a minute."

I trained my field glasses on the balloon and I could see the crew members slapping each other on the back. They thought they had it knocked for sure. But Henry was right. They kept on rising until the balloon was just a tiny speck in the sky. But it was no longer moving forward. We passed right under it as The Head rose into the slipstream and started moving for home. Suddenly the orange balloon started to descend again, but it wasn't coming down slowly. It plummeted toward the earth like a wounded duck.

"They let too much gas out too fast!" said Henry. "You've got to be careful you don't panic when you're rising too fast. It takes a light touch on the release valve. At the rate they're going they'll drop right down through the slipstream again. They might even hit the ground."

Sure enough, the orange balloon kept dropping, seeming to pick up speed as it neared the

157

earth. Its gondola rocked wildly as the rig passed through the slipstream, and we could see the crew frantically dumping sand overboard.

"They'll never make it to Mammoth Falls," Henry observed. "They're dumping a lot of ballast in order to put on the brakes, and they might need it again later on."

The balloon slowed its descent, finally, far beneath us. Then it rose, perhaps a hundred feet, and leveled off. It was moving westward once again, but very slowly. We were two or three miles ahead of it by this time, and moving very fast in the slipstream.

"I think they're finished," said Henry. "Unless they're carrying a lot more ballast that they can get rid of, they'll never get enough altitude to clear the hills around Strawberry Lake."

By now we could see only about ten balloons in the sky. The rest had either foundered on take-off or were too far back to pick up. I finally sighted the Green Onion far to the south of us and at about the same altitude as The Head. Apparently Harmon and his crew had managed to get into the slipstream, too.

There's something about a balloon ride that's different from any other ride on earth. Unless you look down at the ground, you don't even realize you're moving. The balloon goes wherever the wind pushes it, and since you ride right with the wind, there isn't any air rushing past you. It's absolutely quiet and still, and sometimes you feel as though you're just hanging motionless from the sky. Of course, if you get caught in an updraft or a downdraft, or a good storm starts tossing you around, it's a little bit different. But in good, clear weather you can float right over a pasture full of cows and they won't even realize you're there.

Dinky Poore was resting his chin on the railing of our gondola, just daydreaming. It's awfully easy to do that in a balloon, and forget all about the fact you're in a race. I pointed out the location of the Green Onion to Henry. He looked at his watch and checked the map he had tacked to a board.

"I figure we ought to make the fair grounds in a little under two hours, if everything goes well," he said. "The big test comes at Strawberry Lake, when we have to clear those hills. If Harmon's balloon is still with us then, it may be an exciting race."

Just then we got a call on the radio from Jeff. He wanted to know if we could see the Green Onion, and we told him it was off to the south of us, doing pretty well. Just to the north of us, on the main road between White Fork and Mammoth Falls, we could see the long line of cars heading for the fair grounds. With my field glasses I could make out Richard the Deep Breather, chugging along well behind the rest of the caravan. There was a motorcycle escort out in front of the line of cars, and all the candidates for Queen of the County Fair were sitting up on the back seats of convertibles, surrounded by flowers. I couldn't make out which one was Daphne Muldoon.

The radio crackled again, and it was Jeff, telling us that they could see us now, and reminding us that if no balloon could land right on the fair grounds, the crew that could get there first on foot would be declared the winner.

Another voice broke into the transmission. It was Harmon Muldoon, heckling us from the Green Onion.

"If you're gonna run, you'd better get started now, 'cause we're gonna drop right in front of the reviewing stand!"

We looked toward the Green Onion and could see that it had drifted a lot closer to us now. We could see the figures of Harmon and Stony Martin, and Buzzy McCauliffe, the third member of their crew. When I trained the glasses on them, Stony was holding up a sign that said, "Go soak your Head in the lake!"

Dinky Poore started jumping up and down and thumbing his nose at them, and Henry had to tell him to sit down and stop rocking the gondola. In a little while Dinky didn't feel so exuberant, though. We sailed right under a big black cloud, and a summer squall hit us that pitched us around so badly Dinky turned green. He had to lean over the rail for real this time, while I held his legs to keep him from falling out. We were all soaked to the skin, and Dinky sat in two inches of water in the bottom of the life raft, holding his head and mumbling about what he'd do if he ever got back down on the ground again.

When we finally floated out from under that cloud, we'd taken a bad battering and had lost some altitude, but we were all right. Henry checked the altimeter and the helium gauges and decided to let more gas into the envelope of The Head. I climbed up in the rigging and released the sliding yoke to let the bag expand as the gas flowed into it. Henry let the gas out of the pressure tanks carefully. We just needed enough extra lift to get us back up into the slipstream. Too much, and we'd rise right through it!

When we had leveled off again, and were getting a good wind, Henry told Dinky to keep his eye on the altimeter. "We're going to start rising again as soon as we dry out and lose some of the water we've taken on. We'll have to pump that extra gas back into the tanks again to stay in the slipstream."

"What about what *I* lost?" asked Dinky.

"Every ounce counts," said Henry. "I'll let you know if we want you to get sick again."

Now that we were out of the squall, we took a quick look around to take stock of the competition. Only three balloons were in sight. One was the Green Onion, far out ahead of us and heading for the hills east of Strawberry Lake. She had either missed the squall completely or just passed through the edge of it. The other two were closer to us and at lower altitude, neither of them moving as fast as we were. One was painted like a top, with red, white, and blue stripes, and the other was the one that looked like a green caterpillar. If there were any others still aloft, they were too far back to worry about.

"That caterpillar will be lucky to make it to the hills," said Henry. "She's been losing altitude ever since we got started, and I'll bet she's already thrown away all her ballast. I saw them

162

dumping sand just before we went into the squall."

"What about the Green Onion?" I asked. "She must be two miles ahead of us."

"I've got an idea!" he answered while he worked furiously with a pencil on the back of the map board. "Yes, it ought to work. I think we can pass her at Strawberry Lake, if the air currents are moving the way they should be moving."

"I hope you're right," I said. "It looks pretty hopeless right now."

"Gaining altitude, oh Great One!" Dinky Poore sang out. The sunshine and a little fresh air had brought his spirits back.

"Start the compressor!" said Henry. "We'll have to keep pumping a little gas back into the tanks as we dry out."

I cranked up the little gasoline engine and the compressor started to throb. Then I went up in the rigging again to adjust the yoke as the gas seeped back into the pressure tanks.

"Keep your eye on the Green Onion when she reaches the hills this side of the lake," Henry explained. "That ridge of hills creates a tremendous updraft. And when it meets the warm air rising from the lake, it becomes a regular funnel. If the Green Onion tries to cross the ridge in the slipstream, she'll get caught in that funnel and she may zoom up to ten thousand feet. If we play it just right we can slip in under her and beat her across the lake."

"I don't know how you're gonna do it, but I hope you're right!" I said.

"Leave it to Henry!" said Dinky Poore.

"A lot depends on how fast we can pump gas in and out of the bag to vary our lift," said Henry. "We've got to drop down out of the slipstream just before we reach the hills and go in low and heavy. Then, if we're lucky, that updraft should catch us and pop us over the ridge. If it does, we may be home free if we can get enough gas back into the bag fast enough to keep from dropping down the other side and into the lake."

"I hope you know what you're doing," I said, not quite sure of what Henry had in mind.

"Lead on, oh Great One!" said Dinky Poore with supreme confidence.

The Green Onion was now approaching the hills a little over a mile ahead of us. She was sailing high and proud. But Henry had predicted the course of events with uncanny accuracy. Just as she was about to cross the ridge, she veered upward and started to climb at an amazing rate.

"She's caught in the funnel!" Henry shouted.

"Start the compressor again, Charlie. I want to lose at least eight hundred feet and come in well under that ridge."

The little gasoline engine whirred again, and soon we were dropping down out of the slipstream. Henry had timed it just right. We still had plenty of forward momentum; but if we continued dropping at the rate we were, we would crash right into the middle of the hills.

"Don't get sick now, Dinky!" Henry warned. "We need all the weight we have for another minute."

Off to our left we could see the big green caterpillar far below us. It bumped into the lower slopes of the hills and slid into a gully, where it stayed, rocking back and forth in the wind, while its crew tried frantically to get it airborne again. The red, white, and blue top was not much better off. The updraft had caught it, but too late, and it crashed into the upper slope of one huge hill, where it snagged itself among the trees.

"They're finished!" said Henry matter-of-factly. "Shut off the compressor, Charlie, and keep your fingers crossed."

I shut off the engine and stood ready at the pressure tanks to let gas back into the envelope if Henry gave the signal. In a few seconds we had stopped losing altitude and were being blown in toward the side of a hill, swinging and swaying crazily. For one brief moment it looked as though we would surely crash. Dinky Poore's eyes were the size of overcoat buttons, and his face looked like white paste. I guess mine did too, but I couldn't see it. Henry stood leaning against the gondola railing with his arms folded, looking intently at the hill rushing toward us. He seemed to be counting to himself under his breath. He was the complete scientist — intent only on the outcome of his experiment.

Suddenly our downward plunge slackened abruptly and we felt the rush of warm air past our faces. We were so close to the face of the hill that we could have jumped out if we wanted to. The gondola swung like a pendulum as we changed direction and started to rise again. We were in the updraft.

"A little gas, Charlie!" Henry shouted, and I opened the valves for a few critical seconds. "That's enough. Knock it off now!" We were climbing steeply, just swinging clear of the tree-tops. Dinky Poore's eyes started to go back to normal, and we all let out a gasp of relief.

"We've got to watch it at the top," Henry said quickly. "The hill is a lot steeper there and we don't want to get caught in the mainstream of this updraft. The trick is to just sneak over the ridge as low as we can."

The Green Onion was still sailing upward, caught helplessly in the thermal funnel that roared up from the east end of the lake, but there wasn't time to watch her now. We were too busy saving our own skins.

We were just about a hundred feet from the crest of the hill when we suddenly stopped rising and dipped downward with a jolt. It was like being in a fast-rising elevator when it stops suddenly and the floor drops out from under you.

"We've slipped out of the updraft," Henry shouted. "We're going to — "

But the thud of the gondola as it banged against the steep upper slope of the hill bit the words off in his mouth. The Head bounced away from the slope, swayed drunkenly for a moment, then dipped suddenly again, and banged once more against the side of the hill. This time the gondola bounced and slid crazily down the slope. We were too heavy to stay aloft without the help of the updraft.

Henry grabbed Dinky Poore by the shoulders. "Jump out!" he shouted.

Dinky scrambled over the side and dug his toes

and fingers into the shale of the hillside to break his slide. The Head bounced free of the slope once more and hung there precariously for a few anxious seconds. Then, very slowly, it started to drift perceptibly upward. Henry uncoiled the rope ladder hanging on the side of the gondola and flung one end of it over the side toward Dinky.

"Grab that and run up the hill!" he shouted.

Dinky snared one rung of the ladder, hooked it in the crook of his arm, and started clambering over the boulders and scrub growth toward the top of the slope. The Head drifted slowly above him like a huge umbrella, dwarfing his tiny figure with its broad shadow. Henry took his horn-rimmed glasses off and wiped them methodically on the tail of his shirt.

"I think we've got it made," he said, as he put the spectacles back on.

Then he took up the slack in the rope ladder and shouted down to Dinky. "Tie it around you and get ready to climb back up when I give you the signal."

Dinky wrapped the end of the ladder around him and stuck both arms through it, so it was laced across his chest and back. Then he grabbed a rung higher up and stood ready to climb.

"Shoot the gas to her, Charlie, but not too much," Henry told me.

I opened the valves and let more gas back into the envelope. The Head responded and started to climb more rapidly. We had topped the crest of the hill and could see Strawberry Lake on the other side of the next ridge. Dinky came up the ladder like a squirrel, and we heaved him over the side and into the gondola. He was grinning like a circus clown and hollering, "Go get 'em, White Cloud!" We rose rapidly into the slipstream again and picked up speed. We had slipped over the ridge without getting caught in the funnel, and were on the homestretch.

We all looked up now, trying to pick up the Green Onion. She was a tiny speck in the sky far above us, and not much closer to Mammoth Falls. All the time we had been working our way over the ridge, the Green Onion had been going practically straight up. If the wind we were riding held up, we would be 'way out ahead of her in a few minutes. But as it happened, it made no difference.

The speck in the sky suddenly grew larger. The Green Onion had slipped out of the funnel and was plunging toward the earth like a wounded pigeon. Henry grabbed the field glasses out of my hand and tracked the balloon in its descent.

"They're in trouble for sure," he said, after a minute. "Harmon has let too much gas out of the bag. I can tell by the wrinkles in it. That's a bad mistake! When you're caught in an updraft in a free balloon, all you can do is ride it out. If you let a lot of gas escape, you don't have enough lift left to hold you up when the updraft stops pushing you."

"What's gonna happen now?" asked Dinky.

"They'll slow down some, because the farther they drop the denser the air gets. But at the rate they're going, they'll dunk in the lake, for sure!"

Henry called Jeff Crocker on the radio and told him to alert the lake patrol for a possible rescue.

"Start the compressor again," he told me. "We're gonna have to drop down low over the lake, and if we're lucky we might be able to help them."

"Nuts to them!" said Dinky Poore. "We wanna win the race."

"Maybe nobody'll win this race," said Henry. "You start checking the release lines for the life raft. We may have to drop it to them, if we can get close enough."

170

We had our life raft rigged so we could cut it loose in a hurry if we needed it ourselves or if we wanted to get rid of its weight. The heavy tarpaulin that formed the walls and floor lining of our gondola would serve us well enough if we had to jettison the raft.

We all had our eyes fastened on the Green Onion as we settled down over the lake. Harmon and his crew were throwing everything conceivable overboard in a frantic effort to slow the speed of their descent. Shirts, shoes and socks, and even trousers came flying over the side of their gondola to splash in the lake. But it was all to no avail. The Green Onion plummeted into the water like a dead duck.

The force of the impact toppled the gondola on its side, spilling Stony Martin and Buzzy McCauliffe into the water. Harmon Muldoon clung to the rigging and rode with the balloon as it skidded across the surface of the lake, until the weight of the sunken gondola brought it to a stop. We were heading right for it when I shut off our compressor and we leveled off, drifting slowly about fifty feet above the surface.

"Cut the raft loose!" Henry shouted.

We all hit the release lines, and the life raft plopped into the lake about a hundred yards from where the heads of Stony Martin and Buzzy McCauliffe had bobbed to the surface. They both heard it hit the water and started swimming toward it. Henry was uncoiling the rope ladder again.

"Get ready to let more gas into the bag!" he told me, tersely. "And when I give you the signal, give her plenty. We're going to try and pick Harmon up, and until we get him clear of the water he's going to be plenty heavy."

Henry threw the ladder over the side and shouted to Harmon to swim for it. We were still about two hundred yards from him. He was clinging to the shrunken gas bag that had been the Green Onion. It was now a small bubble of green silk, still visible above the surface of the water, but it had drifted far to our left. It was touch-and-go whether Harmon could intercept the rope ladder as it bounced and splashed through the water.

We kept our fingers crossed for the next minute as Harmon swam through the water with strong strokes. Henry paid out all the slack on the ladder that he could, and Harmon got there in time to snag it with an outstretched arm. The effect on The Head was immediate. We dipped sharply downward, and I opened the gas valves without waiting for Henry's signal. We must have come within ten feet of the water before The Head shook violently and veered upward, pulling Harmon clear of the water.

"Good work, Charlie!" Henry cried. "Hang in there, Harmon, and we'll let you down on shore!"

We could see one of the motorboats of the lake patrol starting out from the far shore to pick up the life raft and its occupants. The Head sailed serenely onward under its added load, with Harmon clinging to the lower rungs of the ladder. When we reached the sandy beach on the west shore of the lake, Henry cut the ladder loose and Harmon plopped onto the sand. A baked bean sandwich hit the beach right beside him, and Dinky Poore hollered over the side of the gondola, "Just in case you don't make it back in time for lunch!"

We rose rapidly again, clearing the trees and the low hills on the west side of the lake. We could see the fair grounds dead ahead of us. Henry and I scanned the horizon for signs of the other balloons. We could see three of them still in the air, but they were all far back of us on the other side of the ridge of hills. Unless the sky fell in, we had it made.

As soon as we were over the last ridge of hills we started pumping gas out of The Head at intervals and tightening the yoke up to decrease her size, so that we could lose altitude gradually and glide right in to the fair grounds. With Henry giving the commands, we made a perfect landfall and skimmed in over the heads of the crowd about fifteen feet off the ground. We threw out mooring lines, and about a hundred people tried to get hold of them and tow us up to the officials' stand.

The band had started playing as soon as we were sighted coming over the hills from the lake. It was still going full blast with the "Washington Post March"; and with the crowd yelling and cheering, and fireworks going off all around us, the noise was deafening. The balloon was being pulled in all directions at once by the crowd, and the pitching and tossing of the gondola got so bad that Dinky started to turn green again. Pretty soon he slipped quietly over the side and disappeared among the press of people surging around us. Finally Chief Putney and Constable Billy Dahr managed to fight their way to the side of the gondola, and escorted us with some semblance of order up to the officials' stand.

Mayor Scragg was waving his hat and beaming at the crowd, and Daphne Muldoon stood beside him loaded down with flowers. She was blushing, and trying to keep from giggling, and worrying about the wind blowing her hair; but she managed to hold still long enough for them to put a crown on her head.

When the speechmaking and the band music were all over, we looked around for Dinky Poore. We found him sitting in the back of Zeke Boniface's truck, talking to some reporters from the mammoth Falls *Gazette*. One of them asked him if he wanted to be an astronaut when he grew up, but Dinky shook his head.

"No!" he said. "I think maybe I'd like to be a railroad engineer — or maybe just a movie actor."

"Something's wrong with him," said Freddy Muldoon. "I had to eat his lunch for him, and he doesn't even want a milk shake!"

The Voice in the Chimney

Dinky Poore wrinkled his freckled nose and scroonched his eyes up into tiny slits so he could see better. He pointed along the dusty road to where it curved over the brow of Blueberry Hill.

"Isn't that your cousin Harmon throwing rocks at the old Harkness house? Look! There's a bunch of girls with him."

Freddy Muldoon shaded his eyes with his pudgy hand and looked where his friend was pointing. The chimneys and gables of the abandoned Harkness mansion stood out against the cloudy sky through a gap in the trees that covered most of Blueberry Hill. In the clearing in front of the tall-windowed old house Freddy could see the figures of his cousin Harmon and a group of girls. Sure enough, Harmon was throwing stones up onto the broad veranda and shaking his fist at the silent walls of the house.

"Yeah! That's him, all right," he said. "I wonder what that nut's doin' now. Let's sneak around through the woods and see if we can get up close enough to spy on 'em."

No sooner had he said it than he and Dinky were scrambling over the low stone wall at the side of the road and beating it through the woods to circle around behind the old house that had stood lonely and empty since old Simon Harkness had died there ten years ago.

Old Man Harkness had been a mean old critter, if you could believe all the stories about him. He was one of those people who seem to take pleasure in causing trouble for others. Because he had a lot of money, everybody put up with him and made excuses for his meanness, but nobody really liked him. Even after he was dead he was still able to cause trouble. Nobody could figure out his will, and the relatives who were supposed to inherit all his money have been fighting over it ever since. That's why the rambling old mansion he built still stands unoccupied on Blueberry Hill and is slowly going to pieces.

In the summertime a lot of blueberry pickers eat their picnic lunch on the grounds of the old estate, and the kids rummage through the dusty, creaky rooms of the empty house when the old-sters aren't watching. In the wintertime almost nobody goes near it. Billy Dahr, the town constable, is supposed to drive out and check on it once in a while; but he can't possibly watch it all the time, so gradually the house gets torn apart and people steal things out of it.

When Dinky and Freddy got around behind the house, they crawled up through the bushes to peek through the bars of the ornate iron fence that surrounds it. There was Harmon, with his sister Daphne and three other girls, standing knee-deep in the wiry grass that had once been the most beautiful front lawn in Mammoth Falls.

Harmon aimed a rock at a second-storey window that had a board broken off it, and let fly. The rock fell short and landed with a thud on the veranda roof. Harmon shook his fist at the house and shouted, "Come out and fight like a man, you lousy old ghost!"

Then he turned around and grinned, and the girls all screamed and pretended to be scared.

"What a ninny!" said Dinky.

"Ditto!" said Freddy.

Harmon threw another rock. This one bounced off the window jambs and came tumbling back down onto the lawn. Then Harmon ran up onto the front porch of the house, jumped up and down a few times, waved his arms wildly, and shouted again at the weathered shingles and boarded-up windows. Then he turned around with his back to the house, to show he wasn't scared, and stood there grinning at the girls with his hands on his hips.

"What a jerk!" said Freddy.

"Ditto!" said Dinky.

"Harmon, you come down off there!" one of the girls shouted. "You can't tell what might happen."

"Aw, nuts," said Harmon. "You girls are just scared."

Then, just to show how brave he was, Harmon ran right up to the front door and gave it a vicious kick. You could see he hurt his big toe pretty good when he did it, and a hollow booming sound echoed through the walls of the old house. A slate shingle shook loose from the roof and cascaded down onto the roof of the porch, where it broke into splinters with a loud crack. Harmon turned and dashed off the front porch; but he wasn't looking where he was going, and he tripped over a loose floor board and fell headlong down the steps. He skinned one knee pretty good, but he acted as if it was nothing at all and stood there shaking his fist at the house. He didn't turn his back on it any more, though.

The girls screamed and giggled again, and one of them said, "Let's get out of here. I'm scared!"

"O.K.!" said Harmon, not one to hang around any longer than necessary. "If you're really scared, we'll go back to town. But I'm coming back out here tonight."

"How do you like that?" said Freddy Muldoon behind his hand.

"What a faker!" said Dinky Poore.

"I've always wanted to haunt a house!" said Henry Mulligan, when Freddy and Dinky told us what they had seen out at the Harkness mansion that morning. We were sitting in our clubhouse in Jeff Crocker's barn. Henry had leaned his chair back against the wall, and with his hands thrust in his pockets he was gazing at the rafters. We kept our mouths shut until he had let his chair fall forward again.

"Well?" said Jeff Crocker, who had been whittling himself a whistle from a willow twig all the time Henry had been thinking.

"Homer Snodgrass is pretty skinny, isn't he?" Henry asked.

We all agreed that Homer was pretty skinny, except Homer, who wasn't there.

"I think he'd make a first-rate skeleton!" said Henry. And that was how the Mad Scientists' Club got involved in the mystery of the Harkness house. Before the sun had set that afternoon we had lugged half the equipment in our laboratory out to the old mansion and had set to work to make it as hospitable as possible for Harmon's visit that night.

The Harkness house was an ideal place to haunt. It was built about a hundred years ago, when houses were large and roomy, and it was full of fireplaces and chimneys. Later on the family had installed a central heating system. The huge hot-air furnace that occupied half of one end of the musty basement looked like a giant octopus. Hot-air ducts radiated from it in every direction. They ran through the floors and walls of the old house to every room, and they were big enough for a man to crawl through. There were false ceilings, hidden cupboards, and old-fashioned laundry chutes that ran all the way from the upstairs halls to the basement. And a dumbwaiter that still worked hung in a shaft that reached from the kitchen all the way up to the third-floor bedrooms.

"What a place for ghosts!" said Jeff Crocker, after we had explored the place from top to bottom.

"I think we can give Harmon a reasonably good reception," said Henry Mulligan.

Then Henry started giving orders. By the time it was dark we had the place pretty well bugged. Dinky Poore was slung in a seat down the huge central chimney of the house to a point where the main flue from the furnace entered it. From here he could make ghost calls the echoed through the hot-air registers into every room of the house. Homer Snodgrass had to stand still while Henry and Jeff stuck strips of luminescent tape on him to form the outline of a skeleton. Mortimer Dalrymple put on a sheet that had been dipped in luminescent paint, and tied it tight around his neck. When the two of them stepped in front of the black-light lamps that Freddy and I were rigging up, they gave off an eerie green glow that looked like something out of this world. Mortimer looked like a headless ghost, since you couldn't see his face at all in the black light; and Homer looked as though he belonged in a grave. Jeff gave him a pair of castanets to practice with, so he could make rattling noises as he went through the movements of a skeleton dance he had invented.

We mounted one of the ultraviolet lamps so that it shone on the balcony that ran across one end of the Harkness living room. This was to be Homer's stage for his skeleton dance. The other light we directed at the top of the wide, curving stairway that dominated the entrance hall of the house. This was where Mortimer would do his ghost act. Henry could control both lights from a second-floor closet, where he and Jeff set up an operations center to direct everything we did. With a couple of peepholes bored in the wall they could see into both the living room and the downstairs hall, because both of them were two stories high.

Freddy Muldoon was detailed to the attic, where he was supposed to drag chains across the floor and make other acceptable ghost noises whenever Henry called him on the intercom. My job was to operate the dumb-waiter and raise what havoc I could by moving from floor to floor in it. I could also get from the third floor all the way to the basement in no time by using the rope ladder we'd hung in the big laundry chute.

True to his boast, Harmon Muldoon showed up that night, and what followed was pure panic. He had Stony Martin and Buzzy McCauliffe with him for moral support, and we could hear them breaking into the house through a cellar window. We kept quiet while they inched their way up the cellar stairs, and we let them roam around the first-floor rooms and shine their flashlights around until they got overconfident. Then Freddy started to drag a chain across the floor of the attic, and Dinky began to make a weird moaning sound from his perch in the chimney.

Harmon and his friends started for the cellar stairs, but before they got there the noise had stopped. Then it started again, and I could hear them holding a whispered conference in the main hall. They finally screwed up their courage and started to sneak quietly up the main stairway. Just then the big portrait of Simon Harkness that hung over the fireplace in the living room fell to the door with a crash. Harmon and his friends dashed back down the steps and shone their flashlights around the living room. Two more pictures fell off the walls, and they almost jumped out of their skins. Buzzy McCauliffe flashed his light along the wall where one picture had dropped. He examined the picture and the wall above it.

"Hey, Harmon!" he said in a loud whisper. "There is no way to hang this picture up."

"The hook probably fell out of the wall," said Harmon. "Forget it!"

"It wasn't hanging on a hook," said Buzzy. "There's no wire on the back of the picture."

"Forget it!" said Harmon.

"This sure is a creepy place," Buzzy observed, dropping the picture onto the floor.

Just then the skeleton of Homer Snodgrass danced across the balcony at the end of the room. Buzzy caught sight of it out of the corner of his eye.

"Yipes!" he shouted, and flashed his light across the balcony. There was nothing there.

"What's the matter with you?" asked Harmon.

"I saw a ghost up there on that balcony!"

Harmon flashed his light into the balcony. "You're nuts!" he said. "Stop trying to scare us to death. And keep your voice down."

"I saw a ghost!" Buzzy insisted.

Stony Martin snorted in disbelief. "What kind of a ghost?"

"Smells like rotten eggs," said Harmon, sniffing the air. "There must be something dead around here."

"I told you I saw a ghost," said Buzzy.

Down in the cellar, I threw a little more sulphur powder onto the tiny fire in the furnace grate and scrambled back up the ladder in the laundry chute to the first floor.

"Phew-wee! It's getting worse," said Harmon Muldoon, flashing his light along the wall. "It seems to be coming from this head register. I'll bet there's something dead in the basement."

Something rattled along the balcony at the end of the room, and all three turned in time to see the glowing skeleton of Homer Snodgrass disappear behind the balustrade. Harmon Muldoon let out a bellow, and all three of them bolted from the room into the hall. There, at the top of the great staircase, floated a headless ghost, glowing faintly in the invisible black light. It seemed to be suspended in the air, with no feet under it, as it swayed slowly from side to side in a macabre dance.

The smell of burning sulphur was overpowering now, and a mournful sigh, which seemed to come from every direction at once, echoed through the empty rooms of the house. The rattle of castanets on the livingroom balcony again made it too much for Harmon and his friends. They made for the cellar stairs in a headlong rush. As they passed the dumb-waiter shaft in the kitchen, I stuck a broomstick out through a hole in the wall and caught Buzzy McCauliffe flat on the ankles. He spread-eagled on the floor with a crash, picked himself up, and beat both Harmon and Stony to the door.

"A big black thing just tried to grab me!" he shouted over his shoulder as he flew past them down the cellar stairs and out the window they had forced open.

If any of the three looked back at the house as they fled across the yard and down Blueberry Hill Road, they would have seen a dim lantern swinging back and forth in the windowed cupola atop the house, where it is said old Simon Harkness used to sit for hours peering through a telescope just to see what his neighbors were doing and whether anyone was trespassing on his property. After we got through laughing, we packed up our gear and went home.

Before long, the town of Mammoth Falls was alive with rumors that the Harkness house was haunted for sure. Several times during the next week the swinging light was seen at night high in the cupola. But passers-by who observed it just hurried by the place and were reluctant to tell their friends what they had seen. Nobody went near the place at night. But there is something about a haunted house that human beings just can't resist, and a lot of people snooped around it in the daytime and peeked through cracks in the boarded-up windows and dared each other to go inside.

Finally Chief Harold Putney ordered Constable Billy Dahr to go out and check the house thoroughly and investigate the rumors of unearthly phenomena. Chief Putney said he would like to do it himself, but he had an important date to play golf with Mayor Scragg. Billy Dahr asked if it was all right if he did it in the daytime, and Chief Putney said, "Of course! You can't see anything at night!"

When we heard this we held a council in Jeff Crocker's barn to figure out what we should do.

"I don't wanna do my ghost act," said Mortimer Dalrymple. "I might get arrested for having no visible means of support."

"Very funny!" said Jeff Crocker. "You couldn't do it in daylight anyhow. Billy Dahr is going to be out there this afternoon!"

Since Billy Dahr represented the law, he didn't have to break into the Harkness house. He plodded up the front steps in his oversized policeman's coat and pried two of the boards loose from the front door. Then he inserted a key in the lock and stepped inside. After a quick glance around, he was about to step out again when a scratching noise attracted his attention. It seemed to come from the fireplace in the living room. Constable Dahr crept noiselessly to the living-room door and peered cautiously inside, wagging his billy stick behind him the way he does when he's walking his beat in the Town Square.

"Who's there?" he said, not loud enough for anyone to hear him.

Since there was no answer he turned toward the front door again with a *hrrmph*. As he did so, every picture fell from the living-room walls and crashed to the floor. Billy Dahr spun around like a startled rabbit. He peered into the living room with his eyes popping. Slowly he circled the room, examining each picture carefully and scrutinizing the walls above them. Then he stood in the center of the room scratching his head. The sound of a clanking chain came from the attic, and a stove lid from the old coal stove in the kitchen clattered to the floor. Billy Dahr dashed into the hall, then padded softly toward the kitchen.

While he was creeping down the hall, I slipped into the living room through the other door and hung the pictures back on the wall. The gag was really quite simple. Henry had planted an electromagnet in the wall behind each picture, and taped a steel plate to the back of each frame. Whenever he cut off the current to the magnets, the pictures would fall.

The scratching noise in the chimney brought Billy Dahr back into the living room again. He stood there goggle-eyed, twitching his mustache from side to side Then he pussyfooted up to the fireplace and peered intently at the portrait of Simon Harkness. The portrait fell right at his feet, and he jumped back to the middle of the room waving his billy club in the air. Slowly, he backed out into the hall with his eyes sweeping the walls of the room. No sooner had he turned his back than the other pictures crashed onto the floor.

This was enough for Billy Dahr. He started for the front door, but the creaking noise of the dumb-waiter rising in its shaft stopped him once again. Holding his billy club in front of him he tiptoed back toward the kitchen. There was a tapping sound coming from the door to the dumb-waiter. Billy sneaked up on it with his handcuffs in one fist and his club in the other. He pressed his ear to the door and listened for a moment. Then he flung the door open and jumped back with a loud, croaking scream. Hanging by the neck from the bottom of the dumb-waiter was the figure of a man.

Billy Dahr lost no time in getting out of there and into town to make his report to Chief Putney. He found him on the golf course with Mayor Scragg and brought both of them back out to the Harkness house. By this time we had cut the store-window dummy loose from the dumb-waiter and restored everything to order. Constable Dahr had a hard time convincing Chief Putney and Mayor Scragg that there was anything wrong. They trooped through the whole house, and when they had finished, Chief Putney looked at Billy Dahr with a cold-eyed stare.

"When was the last time you had a vacation?" he asked him.

"I don't rightly know," said Billy Dahr, pushing his cap to one side with the end of his billy club. "Mebbe eight years ago, when I took the missus to Bear Lake."

Chief Putney looked at Mayor Scragg, and Mayor Scragg looked at Billy Dahr. "I quite agree," said the Mayor. "Constable Dahr ought to take a long rest."

"Take a long-g-g rest! Take a long-g-g rest!" sighed a voice in the chimney.

"That's right! I quite agree," said the Mayor.

"What was that?" snapped Chief Putney, striding into the living room.

"What was what?" asked the Mayor.

"I could swear I heard a voice come from that chimney."

"Probably just a chimney swallow," laughed the Mayor.

"More than a swallow. It was a whole sentence."

"Maybe *you* need a rest, Harold," said Mayor Scragg, beaming. "Your golf game hasn't been so good lately."

"It doesn't have to be, as long as I play against you!" said the Chief.

"Well, let's get out of here," said the Mayor, moving toward the door. "Obviously this place isn't haunted."

"I'm not so sure now," said Chief Putney, scratching his chin. "I'm beginning to think Constable Dahr wasn't just seeing things after all."

"Oh, pooh!" said the Mayor. "You're letting your imagination run away with you."

"Would you like to make a small bet on it?"

"Well, I'm not a betting man," returned the Mayor "but if you're silly enough to think this house is actually haunted, I wouldn't mind making a small wager. Shall we say five dollars?"

"No! We won't say five dollars, and I didn't say the house was haunted. I just said that I didn't think Billy Dahr was seeing things. Something is going on here. I just want to bet you won't stay in this house overnight."

"A steak dinner?"

"A steak dinner!"

"You're on!" laughed the Mayor. "Nobody will ever say that Alonzo Scragg was afraid of ghosts!"

Late that night we watched as a police car pulled up before the front steps of the house. Chief Putney escorted Mayor Scragg up onto the veranda and unlocked the door. The Mayor stepped inside, with a sleeping bag under one arm and a lantern in his hand.

"You don't mind if I lock you in, do you?" asked Chief Putney. "I wouldn't want you to lose your bet." Before the Mayor could answer him, he had stepped outside and turned the key in the lock.

From the cupola on top of the roof, where I was keeping watch, I could see the police car pull away from the house. It drove down Blueberry Hill Road for a short distance; then it pulled off to the side and the lights went out. I was pretty sure Chief Putney and Constable Billy Dahr were coming back to the house. I sneaked downstairs to alert Jeff and Henry.

Sure enough, the Chief and Billy Dahr crawled into the cellar through the same window that Harmon Muldoon had broken open. We listened intently to see if we could keep track of their movements through the house, but there was no sound. Apparently they had decided to wait quietly in the basement until Mayor Scragg had settled himself for the night.

"What'll we do now?" I whispered to Jeff. "We don't wanna get arrested."

"Play it cool!" Jeff whispered back. "We know they're here, but they don't know we're in the house. We'll just play it close to the chest."

Meanwhile Mayor Scragg had settled himself in a corner of the living room. His lantern was set on the floor, and in the dim island of light around it Jeff and Henry could see him puffing air into the rubber mattress of his sleeping bag. I let myself down in the dumb-waiter and made a noise like shuffling feet in the kitchen. When Mayor Scragg crept down the hall to investigate, I sneaked in through the door from the dining room, blew out his lantern and let all the air out of his mattress again. Then I tiptoed upstairs and climbed quietly down the big laundry chute to eavesdrop on the two in the basement.

At first all I could hear was Chief Putney complaining about not being able to smoke a cigar. Then I heard them talking in hoarse whispers about how they might scare the wits out of Mayor Scragg so Chief Putney could collect his bet. Finally, after a long wait, I heard them move over to the giant furnace. They flashed their lights around inside it. Then they started to investigate the hot-air ducts that led from it to the first-floor rooms. They located one of the big ones leading to the living room and traced it back to the furnace. Chief Putney opened the access door in the rear of the furnace cowling. It was large enough for a man to get inside to clean out the air ducts. He whispered some instructions in Billy Dahr's ear and stuffed him inside. Then he started making his way quietly up the stairs that led to the kitchen.

I could hear Billy Dahr crawling along the air duct leading to the living room. As soon as Chief Putney had reached the top of the stairs I dropped out of the laundry chute and softly closed the access door in the rear of the furnace. It couldn't be opened from the inside, and unless somebody let him out, Billy Dahr was trapped in the heating system for the night.

I was making my way up the rope ladder in the laundry chute again when bedlam broke loose. A sound of violent coughing echoed through the house, followed by choking cries for help. It sounded like Dinky Poore.

When I got to the second floor I scrambled out into the hall and ran to the balcony that over-looked the living room. Mayor Scragg had found some wood in the kitchen and had kindled a fire in the huge fireplace. He was standing in front of it, trying to peer up into the chimney to see what was going on. Every time he'd open the draft to let the smoke go up the chimney, it would bang closed again. He was coughing and spitting and trying to wave the smoke away from his face. I knew if we didn't do something fast Dinky would be a cooked goose.

I turned and ran for the stairs to the attic. Just then Homer Snodgrass rattled across the balcony in his glowing skeleton costume and make a gur-gling noise in his throat. Mayor Scragg bolted from the room and out into the hall. There was the headless ghost, dancing at the top of the stair-case. This time it didn't stay there, but moved menacingly down the stairs until Mayor Scragg panicked and ran for the kitchen. He burst through the swinging door, knocking Chief Put-ney flat on the floor, and pounded on the door to the back porch. It was locked fast, and boarded up to boot. He circled the kitchen blindly, looking for a way out, and stumbled on the door to the dumb-waiter. Flinging it open, he climbed inside and pulled it closed after him.

Chief Putney was writhing on the kitchen floor, gasping for breath. He never did know who came through the swinging door.

Mortimer Dalrymple retreated to the upstairs hall when he heard the commotion in the kitchen. Silhouetted against the window at the end of the hall he could see the figure of Jeff Crocker waving wildly to him. Jeff was standing by the dumb-waiter shaft, and when Mortimer reached him he whispered in his ear, "I think Mayor Scragg climbed into the dumb-waiter. When I open the door, you grab the rope and pull it up about ten feet. Maybe we can catch him between floors."

Jeff popped the door open and Mortimer grabbed the pull rope. Together they heaved on it and knotted it tightly to the main cable. The Mayor of Mammoth Falls was trapped.

Meanwhile I had reached the attic and found Freddy Muldoon. Together we scrambled out onto the roof and dashed to the main chimney. We tugged on the ropes of Dinky's sling seat and lifted him out of the chimney. He was grimy and black, and his eyes were watering, but he was all right. We hustled him into the attic and down to the second floor. Somebody was banging on the wall of the dumb-waiter shaft and hollering for help. From the depths of the basement came the ringing sound of a billy club beating on metal. Jeff and Mortimer loomed out of the shadows.

"Chief Putney is still in the kitchen," Jeff whispered. "He'll be up in a minute to see what the hollering is all about, and we've got to be ready for him."

We could hear him fumbling about in the hall and striking matches. He found Mayor Scragg's lantern and lighted it, then started for the stairs. At the top he could dimly see the headless ghost and the glowing skeleton waltzing with each other. When the light from his lantern struck them, they broke and ran down the hall with a cackle of fiendish laughter echoing after them and Chief Putney in hot pursuit.

Homer ducked behind a bedroom door, but Mortimer continued up the stairs to the third floor, and from there to the attic. Mortimer can run like blazes, but he kept just far enough ahead to let himself be visible in the light of the lantern. When he reached the attic, he flung off his ghost sheet and hooked it to a fishing line tied to a pulley at the top of the steep steps leading to the cupola. Then he dove behind an old trunk while the sheet continued swinging up the stairs into the cupola. Chief Putney charged right up the steps after it, and Freddy Muldoon popped out from behind the door and slammed it closed and locked it. Chief Putney had the cupola all to himself for the night.

"I do believe that house is haunted," said Freddy Muldoon, pointing back over his shoulder as we made our way through the woods toward town. We all looked back, and we could see Chief Putney waving Mayor Scragg's lantern high in the cupola, and we could hear faint sounds of pounding and cries for help.

"You must be some kind of a nut!" said Mortimer Dalrymple. "I don't see anything."

"Neither do I," said Homer Snodgrass.

Very late that night Lem Perkins and Johnny Soames jounced along Blueberry Hill Road in Lem's pickup truck, on their way back from the cattle auction.

"Is that a light on the roof of the old Harkness house?" said Johnny.

"I don't see any light," said Lem.

"Right there!" said Johnny. "On the roof— no, it's gone again. Maybe we ought to stop."

"Some people have a wild imagination," said Lem. "Even if I saw a light I wouldn't believe it. That house hasn't been lived in for years."

"Mebbe you're right," said Johnny. "I guess it doesn't pay to stick your nose into other people's business."

" 'Specially if they're dead!" said Lem. And he gave the old truck all the gas it could take on the bumpy road.

Throughout the night, Mayor Scragg and Billy Dahr pounded in vain, and Chief Putney waved his lantern in the cupola to no avail. They were still doing it when Daphne Muldoon and her friends visited the old house late the next morning and finally let them out.

Chief Putney doesn't investigate any rumors about the Harkness place any more, and Mayor Scragg turns red when anybody mentions it. Most folks in town believe that there never were any ghosts in the place, and that the Mayor and Chief Putney, for some reason, were just trying to scare people away from it.

Night Rescue

"If you want to find a needle in a haystack, you've got to be systematic about it," said Henry Mulligan. "Otherwise it's like looking for a needle in a haystack."

This didn't make much sense to Dinky Poore, who isn't the most brilliant member of our club. But Henry proved he was right, as he always does.

It was the day the Air Force jet fighter exploded over Mammoth Falls. A big search and rescue effort was being organized. But when Henry and I offered the help of the Mad Scientists' Club, Mayor Scragg threw up his hands and told us to keep out of his hair — of which he has almost none.

"We don't need your help," said the Mayor

testily, as he wiped the sweat from his glasses. "Every time you Mad Scientists get mixed up in something it gives me trouble. Why don't you go home and leave me alone?"

"But we have a plan, Mr. Mayor. . . ." Henry ventured.

"I don't think we ought to turn down any offers of help," said a tall man in an Air Force uniform. It was Colonel March, from Westport Field. "If that pilot is still alive he may not last through the night. It's going to get dark pretty soon, and we've got to call off the air search. Let's put these boys to work. I don't see that they can do any harm."

"You don't know *these* boys!" said the Mayor.

"Didn't they say they belong to an Explorer post?" the Colonel asked.

"They call themselves the Mad Scientists of Mammoth Falls. You figure it out, Colonel."

"Our specialty is science, sir," Henry explained. "Jason Barnaby saw the plane explode — right over his apple orchard, up on Brake Hill, while he was plowing."

"We know the pilot got out," said the Colonel. "The ejection seat is missing."

"I have a theory about where he came down,"

Henry said seriously, "but I'd have to perform some experiments, first."

"O.K." The Colonel was smiling. "You go ahead and make your experiments — whatever they are. When you decide where you want to make your search, let me know, so I can coordinate it with the other search parties."

"Yes, sir!" Henry said, smartly.

We headed straight for our science lab in Jeff's barn, with Henry spitting out orders to me.

Henry said he had to stop off at his house to pick up some stuff, so I left him at the corner of Carmel Street and ran on to Jeff Crocker's barn. At the lab I pushed the Panic Button. This sounds a buzzer in the house of every member and it means, "Get over to the clubhouse pronto, Tonto."

Fifteen minutes later Henry showed up with two black cardboard cylinders that he shoved into his knapsack. Everybody else was already there, and Jeff Crocker had us all lined up, checking our equipment.

"Sure took you long enough," Jeff said to Henry. "We're practically ready to go. Only we don't know where."

"I had to call the airport for some important

information," Henry explained. "We're going up on Brake Hill above Jason Barnaby's place."

Henry grabbed Homer Snodgrass and sat him down in front of our ham outfit.

"You've got to stay here near the phone, Homer, so we can contact Search and Rescue Headquarters at the Town Hall, if we have to. They won't let us use their radio frequency. We'll take the portable transmitters with us, and when we get set up on Brake Hill we'll call you."

We have a big map of the whole county on the wall of our clubhouse, with grid squares on it, and Henry put a red circle at the place where we expected to set up operations on the hill so Homer would know where we were.

When we finally got to the top of the hill it was already getting dark. Henry had Dinky and Freddy Muldoon pace off the distance to two large trees he had spotted on the ridge north and south of us. When they got back, Henry made some notes in his notebook. Then he had me spread out a big map, just like the one we have in our clubhouse, and orient it with a compass so that the north indicator on the map pointed exactly north.

We set up the two black cardboard cylinders Henry had brought with him.

"These are Army parachute flares," Henry explained. "They'll go up about a thousand feet and drift with the wind. We can track them with compasses to get a good idea where they come down. I've rigged a little radiosonde transmitter inside each of them. If the flare burns out before they reach the ground, we can still get a compass reading on where they land, with the directional radio receivers."

"Do you think we're going to find this pilot, Henry?" Jeff asked.

"If my calculations are correct, we should find him," Henry answered. "I checked with Westport Field, and the wind is still the same as it was when he bailed out this morning. This flare should at least tell us what direction he drifted. Then I'll have to calculate how far he went before he hit the ground."

A few minutes later Dinky Poore was 'way up in the big oak tree to the north of us with a night compass, and Jeff Crocker sat at the foot of it with one of our directional radio receivers. In the other big tree to the south, Mortimer Dalrymple and Freddy Muldoon were stationed with the same kind of equipment.

Henry walked over to the big rock where he had set up the first flare and pulled off the safety clip. We ducked behind a tree when the flare shot off with a swishing roar, straight up into the sky.

It exploded in a shower of sparks, and a bright red, glowing thing dangled there on the cords of a tiny parachute. It lighted up the whole of the hill and the valley to the west of us, and half the lake could be seen as clear as daylight. The wind began to blow the flare, and it swayed and danced in the sky, getting brighter all the time as it drifted off to the west a little bit north of the lake.

It kept getting smaller and smaller. When it finally went out, Henry ran over to the map and jotted down the last reading he got on his compass. Then he got on the walkie-talkie and talked with Jeff and Mortimer. Both of them said they were still getting a beep from the little transmitter in the flare.

When we were all together again, Henry took down the compass readings each team had gotten, and with a protractor and a ruler he drew these bearings on the map.

"I still don't see how all this bunk is gonna help us find the pilot," grumbled Dinky. "Why don't we go out and start searching?"

"We'll search," said Henry, "but if the experiments work, we'll know *where* to search."

Then Henry really started to work. He sat on a

flat rock with a pencil and slide rule and reams of paper. Pretty soon the ground all around him was littered with paper, but he came out with a point where the pilot was likely to have come down.

It was a point in the hills about six miles west of town, where we all knew there was an old abandoned quarry.

Dinky Poore was sent shinnying up a tall spruce to place a flashing road lantern at the very top of it. Henry said we would use this as a reference point to shoot a back azimuth to, so we could check our bearings on the way. Freddy Muldoon was given the job of staying on Brake Hill with the ham outfit so we could keep in touch with Homer back at the clubhouse. We packed our bedrolls, walkie-talkies, emergency rations, and first-aid supplies on our backs and took off.

The sharp edge of a cliff silhouetted against the stars served as a good landmark to guide us until we got down off the hill and into the woods. Then we could no longer see it. Moving through woods at night without losing direction isn't easy, but Jeff and Henry had it all figured out.

"The important thing," Jeff said, "is to keep checking your direction all the time. When you shoot a compass bearing, pick out a landmark as far away from you as possible. This reduces the chance of making an error. It's just like drawing a straight line on a piece of paper. If you use a long ruler, it's easy. If you use one only two inches long, it's pretty hard to make the line straight."

"What if it's so dark you can't see any landmark at all?" Dinky asked him.

"I'll show you in a few minutes," Jeff said. "We're getting into pretty deep woods right now."

Sure enough, we got into a place so pitch black we couldn't even see each other. Then Jeff gave us a demonstration. He called it "leapfrogging." He sent Mortimer ahead with a flashlight. After he was two or three hundred yards ahead of us, Jeff would holler to him to move either right or left. When his light was right in line with the compass bearing we were supposed to follow, we would all take off to the place where he stood. Then Jeff would send him out ahead of us again.

Sometimes we'd sight back to the light we'd left on Brake Hill, if we could see it. If we couldn't, we'd call Freddy on the radio and have him turn on the radiosonde transmitter so we could tune in on the beep with our directional receiver. This way we could check on how close we were keeping on course.

208

We had a little problem when we got to the creek that tumbles out of Strawberry Lake. We couldn't afford to get our equipment all wet by swimming across, so Jeff found a place where the bank on our side was pretty steep. He slung a length of rope over the bough of a big tree that stuck out over the water, and had us shine our flashlights on the other shore. Then he tore down the bank like Tarzan and swung out over the creek. He landed with a squishy splash just at the water's edge on the other side, knee-deep in mud. But he was all right, and we now had a good stout rope stretched across the stream, as well as a piece of clothesline that Jeff had tied securely to his belt.

Jeff tied the big rope good and taut to another tree on his side and we ferried all our stuff across by hanging it on a loop from the big rope and pulling the clothesline back and forth.

The rest of us went across hand over hand, with the clothesline hooked to our belts as a safety line and the loop slung under our armpits so we couldn't fall if our hands slipped off the rope. We all made it in good style except Dinky. He's so skinny that he slipped right out of the noose when he lost his grip, and we had to pull him out of the water with the clothesline. He was

209

sopping wet and mud from head to foot, and he wanted to go home. But Jeff made him take all his clothes off and we pinned a big blanket around him.

"The best thing to do is to keep moving around when you're all wet, so you can build up plenty of body heat," said Jeff. "Let's move out now. We've got to keep going."

"This stinky old blanket scratches!" said Dinky, sobbing a little bit.

"Scratch it right back!" said Mortimer.

It was just about midnight when we crawled to the top of a low ridge that we figured must be in the area the pilot had drifted to.

We found a small clearing, where we set our gear down and held a council meeting to decide what to do next. First of all, Jeff insisted that we build a fire in the middle of the clearing and bank it up well with a rock and dirt fire wall so it couldn't spread. This would give us a reference point to guide us while we did our scouting, and also would make it easy to get back to the clearing. Besides, Dinky could dry his clothes out and get dressed.

"There's a quarry back there, and we don't know much about it," Jeff said. "Let's get organized before we start."

We decided to tie ourselves together, two and two, with lengths of rope, the way mountain climbers do, and be extra careful. We left Dinky to watch the fire and listen for radio calls from Freddy. Then we set off through the woods.

"When you come to the quarry, don't go too near the edge," Jeff warned. "A piece might crumble off and dump you right to the bottom. Henry and I will go along the left rim, You two go to the right. If you see anything, or find a way down to the bottom, call us on the walkie-talkie."

Roped together, Mortimer and I crept along through the underbrush. At the edge of the quarry we could see Jeff and Henry on the other side shining their flashlights down into the pit. It was so dark we couldn't see much, but it looked as though it was about eighty feet deep and covered with scrub growth on the bottom.

Henry called over the walkie-talkie that he would throw a road flare into the pit. The flare exploded into a big hissing ball of red light that cast eerie, dancing shadows on the quarry walls. We could see that the west end of the quarry was completely blocked off by a huge stagnant pond of rain water that had collected there.

"Look! Look!" shouted Mortimer.

I followed his pointing finger to the quarry

wall on the opposite side. Right below the point where Jeff and Henry stood on the rim we could see the torn shreds and dangling cores of a parachute hanging from a scrub pine that grew out of the face of the wall. Huddled among the limestone boulders at the bottom we would dimly make out a dark shape.

"The pilot!" we shouted at the tops of our lungs. "The pilot's down there!"

The next fifteen minutes went so fast I can't remember all that happened, but Jeff told us to go get Dinky and all the rope we could find and come back to the quarry.

We made a safety line out of the rope and sent Dinky over the edge. We could hear him scrambling around over the boulders at the bottom. Suddenly he shouted up to us. "It's him, all right! It's the pilot!"

"How is he? Is he alive?"

"I don't know," Dinky answered. "It's scary down here!"

We pulled the rope back up, and Jeff went down to the quarry floor. Then we took off to get the rest of our gear. We doused the campfire at the clearing and carried everything to the rim of the quarry.

"The pilot's still alive," Jeff shouted up to us.

"But he's pretty bad off. He's unconscious, and I don't want to move him 'cause he might have a broken back. It's foolish to try and get him out of here."

We decided to move everything to the bottom of the quarry and leave Mortimer up on the rim, where he could keep radio contact with Freddy. While Henry and I worked with the rope sling, Mortimer tried to reach Freddy on the walkie-talkie. A woman answered.

"What's your destination?" she asked.

"Where's Freddy?" Mortimer asked.

"What do you mean, where's Freddy? Who is this? Number Seven?"

"Who are you?"

"This is the Ajax Taxi Company. What do you want?"

"Please get off the air, lady. This is an emergency!"

"You get off the air. We've got a license for this radio."

"Forget the walkie-talkie!" Henry said excitedly. "Hook up the portable ham transmitter. Tune it to one four five point two megacycles. That's the emergency frequency that they're working on. Get the Town Hall direct and tell them exactly where we are."

The next hour and a half we worked like beavers. Henry and Jeff went to work on the pilot while Dinky and I set up camp on the quarry floor. Messages kept coming through on the radio from Search and Rescue Headquarters at the Town Hall.

The pilot had a fracture of the leg. Jeff and Henry made a splint from branches of scrub trees and my shirt. They moved the rocks away from him so he could lie flat on his back, and covered him with blankets. He was in deep shock. Jeff told us to build fires at three widely separated points in the quarry to serve as location markers in case Colonel March wanted to fly a plane over the area to fix our location.

"We can do better than that, Jeff," Henry said. "I've got a surplus weather balloon in my knapsack and a thousand feet of nylon thread. We can fly the balloon with a flashlight tied beneath it, and they'll be able to see it all the way from town."

Henry's knapsack was a regular McGee's closet. He could always pull something out of it you never knew he had.

We had just sent the balloon up when a message came through that they might try to send a small helicopter in before daylight if it was possible to land anywhere nearby. Jeff sent back word that we would clear an area on the quarry floor and let them know when we were ready.

One light plane did fly over, and the pilot saw the balloon and the fires all right, because he circled back and came in very low over the trees. We thought the vibration would shake the walls of the quarry loose when he went overhead. He pulled up sharply and dropped something over the side. It came swinging down on a small parachute and dropped with a big splash in the stagnant pond at the open end of the quarry.

"Come on!" Jeff shouted. "Bring a flashlight."

He crashed through the underbrush and charged right into the pond. I got there just in time to catch the parachute on the surface of the water in the beam of my flashlight, and I plunged right in after Jeff. The pond was a deep pit and we had to swim, but we got to the parachute in time to grab the package before it sank. We got it back to shore and opened it. It contained four flares, some medical supplies and a note. The note told us that if they decided to try a helicopter landing the pilot would circled overhead and drop a parachute flare to light up the area. Then we were to light the flares we had, two yellow and two red, to mark the place the chopper was to land.

Jeff and I were dripping wet, but we soon dried off when we all went to work with hatchets to clear the scrub growth from an area about fifty feet in diameter in the middle of the triangle formed by our three campfires.

It wasn't long before we heard the *putt-putt-putt* of the chopper's motor and the thrashing of its rotor blades. Then we saw its blinking lights over the rim of the quarry and rushed out to set off the flare that marked the circle it was to land in. They sent up huge billowing clouds of red and yellow smoke. It made a beautiful sight as the smoke caught the light of the campfires and the chopper hovered overhead, beating the air with its blades. We could see the pilot and the Air Force doctor looking down at us. The wind from the rotor blades beat our shirts and trousers back against us and made the smoke from the flares swirl around on the ground. The whole quarry floor throbbed as the chopper settled down. We had to turn our backs to it and run for cover to get away from the loose gravel and dust it kicked up and sent flying in all directions.

It took only a minute for the doctor, who was

an Air Force major, to check the jet pilot over thoroughly.

"Somebody did a first-rate job here!" he said quietly. "You probably saved this man's life. Get one of those stretchers over here."

It seemed like a long time, but it probably wasn't more than fifteen minutes before we had the stretcher back on the skids of the chopper and the pilot wrapped snugly in blankets under the protective plastic hood.

The Army pilot inspected everything carefully and radioed in to Westport Field for wind and temperature information. Then he looked slowly around the rim of the quarry, where the dawn was beginning to form a faint halo of light. He rubbed his chin thoughtfully and spoke briefly with the doctor. Then they both walked over to where we were standing.

"How much do you weigh, fella?" the pilot was looking right at Dinky Poore.

Dinky gulped.

"Eighty-five pounds, sir."

"I'm going to need all the help I can get to lift out of here. The Major is too heavy. I need somebody about your weight to ride the other stretcher on my side and help balance the load. Would you like to take a ride?"

"Sure . . . yeah . . . I guess so . . . !" Dinky scratched his head and looked around at the rest of us for encouragement.

Dinky was trembling a little bit when we strapped him onto the other stretcher and put the plastic hood over his head, but it might have been because he was cold.

"Tie me on good," he said.

Just then a call came in on the chopper's radio. It was Colonel March, at Search and Rescue Headquarters, telling the pilot to make sure we stayed in the quarry until daylight. A big H21 helicopter would be over the quarry in about an hour to take us and all our gear back into town. We all gave a cheer when we heard this, and Dinky held up two fingers in the victory sign as the Army pilot revved up his motor.

We lowered Mortimer and our radio equipment down to the quarry floor on the rope sling. Now that the excitement was all over we flopped down on the ground dead tired, and I think most of us fell asleep.

The noise of the giant H21 "Grasshopper" coming in woke me up. Colonel March stepped out of it when it touched down. He shook all our hands and told us the pilot had been flown direct to the Westport Field Hospital, where the doctors said he would live.

The big chopper brought us down in a field back of Town Hall, where tents had been set up for feeding the search teams. Freddy Muldoon was already there, gulping down hot cakes and bacon. Another helicopter had brought him and our ham equipment down off Brake Hill. Dinky Poore was lying on an Army cot sipping lemonade through a straw, while one Air Force nurse held the glass for him and another one treated the blisters on his feet.

When we climbed down out of the helicopter, Mayor Scragg and some of the Town Council were there to greet us, along with most of Colonel March's staff officers from Westport Field. Photographers started taking pictures, and they told us there would be a parade in our honor at the air base the next day.

Mayor Scragg had to make a flowery speech, and Mortimer Dalrymple sneezed all the way through it, because his feet were wet. From what the Mayor said, you'd have thought it was his own idea to send us out on the search. But we didn't really mind, because the Mayor had run home from the Town Hall and put on his best suit for the occasion, and he'd got several of the Council members out of bed to come meet us, so we felt quite flattered by it all.

Besides, Colonel March told us he was recommending that the Department of the Air Force award medals for meritorious service to all the members of the Mad Scientists' Club, and this made us really proud. He also said he hoped we would think about trying for the Air Force Academy when we got ready to go to college, because the Air Force needs plenty of scientists.

We all had some hot breakfast in the Red Cross tent, and then they bundled us into hostess wagons to take us home. Mayor Scragg shook all our hands again and asked us if there was anything the town could do for us.

Freddy Muldoon said, "Yes! How about another plate of fried eggs?"